He ran his hand across her hips and pushed his body more tightly into hers.

Then suddenly his entire body tensed. She looked up at him, but as she opened her mouth to ask what was wrong, he laid a single finger across her lips. Immediately her pulse spiked.

He slipped out of bed and pulled on his jeans and shirt, then retrieved his pistol from the nightstand, where he'd left it earlier. "Stay here and lock the door behind me," he whispered before slipping silently out of the room.

Alaina hurried to the door as quickly as she could without noise. Carter had already disappeared downstairs in the darkness. She strained to make out any sound, but all she heard was her own heartbeat. She knew Carter had heard something, though. He'd gone from erotic god to cop in a split second.

Dear Harlequin Intrigue Reader,

For nearly thirty years fearless romance has fueled every Harlequin Intrigue book. Now we want everyone to know about the great crime stories our fantastic authors write and the variety of compelling miniseries we offer. We think our new cover look complements and enhances our promise to deliver edge-of-your-seat reads in all six of our titles—and brand-new titles every month!

This month's lineup is packed with nonstop mystery in *Smoky Ridge Curse,* the third in Paula Graves's Bitterwood P.D. trilogy, exciting action in *Sharpshooter,* the next installment in Cynthia Eden's Shadow Agents miniseries, and of course fearless romance—whether from newcomers Jana DeLeon and HelenKay Dimon or veteran author Aimée Thurlo, we've got every angle covered.

Next month buckle up as Debra Webb returns with a new Colby Agency series featuring The Specialists. And in November *USA TODAY* bestselling author B.J. Daniels takes us back to "The Canyon" for her special *Christmas at Cardwell Ranch* celebration.

Lots going on and lots more to come. Be sure to check out www.Harlequin.com for what's coming next.

Enjoy,

Denise Zaza

Senior Editor

Harlequin Intrigue

THE ACCUSED

USA TODAY Bestselling Author
JANA DELEON

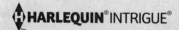

To Christopher Fulbright, for all your support and encouragement. May your own career launch in a spectacular way.

ISBN-13: 978-0-373-69708-3

THE ACCUSED

Copyright © 2013 by Jana DeLeon

Printed in U.S.A.

ABOUT THE AUTHOR

Jana DeLeon grew up among the bayous and small towns of southwest Louisiana. She's never actually found a dead body or seen a ghost, but she's still hoping. Jana started writing in 2001—she focuses on murderous plots set deep in the Louisiana bayous. By day she writes very boring technical manuals for a software company in Dallas. Visit Jana on her website, www.janadeleon.com.

Books by Jana DeLeon

*Mystere Parish
**Mystere Parish: Family Inheritance

CAST OF CHARACTERS

Alaina LeBeau—The attorney thinks the terms of the inheritance will give her an opportunity to consider her career path. She doesn't expect to walk into more trouble than she left behind.

Carter Trahan—Calais's sheriff has no desire to play babysitter based on the ridiculous terms of a crazy woman's will, but because the attorney asking for the favor is his mom's oldest friend, he agrees. Unfortunately, the favor turns out to be anything but simple.

Steven Adams—He made no secret that he blamed Alaina when his daughter fell apart on the witness stand. He can't account for his whereabouts for the past couple of days, and even his wife seems worried about his mental state.

Larry Colbert—The man was certain that if it hadn't been for Alaina LeBeau, his child would still be alive. Now he's missing and Alaina is certain that the restraining order she took out against him won't be enough to keep her safe if Larry wants her dead.

Jack Granger—The Calais local has spent years running errands for the eccentric man holed up in the LeBeau mansion. He's been paid little for his trouble and has continued to do the man's work in return for the promise of inheriting great wealth. If the sisters meet the terms of their mother's will, he'll get nothing.

Kurt McGraw—Alaina's former coworker stole out from under her the partnership she was due, but does he have a reason to get rid of her permanently?

Chapter One

Once upon a time, in a tiny bayou village, there lived a beautiful widow and her three lovely daughters. The woman loved her children and her home, but as time passed, she grew lonely. A handsome and treacherous stranger swept her off her feet and she became a bride for the second time.

But no happily ever after was forthcoming.

Alaina LeBeau stared across the desk at the senior partner of the law firm and struggled to contain her emotions. Finally, anger eclipsed common sense.

"You told me if I got my success rate up, the junior partnership was mine," she said. It was all she could do not to scream at the news that Kurt "Kip" McGraw, an attorney of woefully less skill and somewhat dubious personal reputation, had gotten the partnership she'd been all but assured.

Everett Winstrom III gave her a placating smile. "Now, now. I didn't say it was yours for certain. I merely said if you proved yourself a winner in the courtroom that I felt a partnership would be forthcoming, and I still think one is."

"When would that be exactly? The company is structured to only add a new partner when an existing one retires. All the original partners have been replaced with younger attorneys. It may be twenty years before one of you retires."

"In twenty years, you'll still be a young woman."

"In twenty years, Kurt will be even younger than I, and likely, still as incompetent."

The senior partner gave her another thin, placating smile. "Now, Alaina, you know that the courtroom isn't the only place an attorney makes a good impression on the partners. Kurt has political connections that the firm can take advantage of."

"Based on the news reports and the number of drunk-and-disorderly dismissals we've gained for his political connections, I would guess anyone could take advantage of them."

Everett's jaw tightened and the jovial-uncle act was over. "The fact is, we can't afford to have you as a partner of this firm. Not after the Warren fiasco."

Alaina felt as if she'd been slapped. As if she didn't feel guilty enough over that case, and now the man who'd been her senior adviser was putting all the blame on her?

"I see," she said. "The firm needs a scapegoat and it's not going to be you."

"Did you really think it would be? Someone has to answer for that screwup."

"A child died, Everett. That was far more than a screwup. You can put the blame on me all you want, but we both know we could have prevented what happened."

Anger flashed in the partner's cold, dark eyes. "Nonsense. A psychopath killed that child. That's unfortunate, but it's hardly my fault. You were lead. If there was something missed, that's on you."

Suddenly, Alaina couldn't take another minute of it. The years of busting her butt through law school while working full-time had been small challenge compared to the years of sucking up to these pompous, entitled men who'd never worked for anything other than a more luxurious life.

"Consider this my notice," she said before she could change her mind.

Everett's eyes widened. "Now, let's not be hasty."

"It's something I should have done years ago. I'd hardly call that hasty. In fact, I'd call it a little late in coming. So late that I might have ruined any chance I had at a big career."

"But you're in the middle of three corruption cases—"

"No. *You're* in the middle of three corruption cases. I'm just assisting." As usual, she had been assigned to the anal-retentive detail work of sorting through all the financial information—work that everyone avoided if at all possible and work that she caught far too often. With Everett's analyst on maternity leave, and her giving notice, he'd have no choice but to actually do grunt work for a change.

That thought gave her the sliver of joy that was necessary to smile and stand her ground. "I wish I could say it's been great, Everett, but the reality is, this job has shown me what I don't want to do with the rest of my life. I'll spend the next two weeks completing the paperwork on the cases I've just closed."

His face flushed red and he clenched his hands. "Don't bother. Get your things and get out of this office. I'll mail your final paycheck. You're making a big mistake."

"It's not the first."

She spun around and marched down the hall to her office before he could formulate a reply. A couple of seconds later, she heard the door to his office slam shut. The

firm intern, a studious, humorless girl with an encyclope-
dic recall of law, stepped into her office, her eyes wide.

"Is everything okay, Ms. LeBeau?"

"Everything is perfect, Ms. Jensen. In fact, better than
perfect. I've just given my notice."

"Oh, my... I... Well, if that's what you want to do, then
I'm happy for you, of course." Emily Jensen stared down
at the floor. "I guess you didn't get the partnership."

"No, they gave it to Kurt."

Emily sighed and glanced out into the hallway, then
back at Alaina. "I'm sorry," she said, her voice almost a
whisper. "I don't think that's right."

"If you mean, the person with the most ability didn't
get the job, then I agree. But the reality is, it's their law
firm and Kurt has connections I'll never have. Better to
find out now than spend another seven years here."

Emily nodded. "Don't tell anyone, but I'm only working here to get the experience on my résumé. I intend to
establish my career in nonprofits."

Alaina smiled. "You're a good person. I have no doubt
you're going to accomplish a lot for society with your career."

Emily blushed and she gave Alaina a shy smile. "What
are you going to do now?"

"I don't know exactly. I have money saved. It's not like
I've had much time off to spend it. I may do nothing for
a couple of months and give some serious consideration
to my options."

"I think that's a great idea. You deserve a break." She
handed an envelope to Alaina. "This was addressed to you
personally, not in care of the law firm, so I didn't open it.
I was afraid it wasn't business-related."

"Thanks," Alaina said. "I'm going to miss you, Emily.
Please stay in touch."

"Of course. I'm going to miss you, too, Ms. LeBeau." She left the office and quietly pulled the door shut behind her.

Alaina flopped into her office chair and the first twinge of fear ran through her. *What have you done?* Sure, the job sucked, but it paid well, and given the firm's long history, she had good standing in the legal community.

She sighed. If money and a good reputation were all that mattered, it would be perfect. But the reality was, they weren't the most important things to her. If she was being honest with herself, she'd been fighting discontent for years. Now she was thirty-two years old, and no closer to knowing what she wanted to do with her life than she was when she'd started law school.

It was depressing on so many levels.

She glanced down at the envelope lying on her desk and frowned. The return address was for a law firm, but wasn't one she recognized as related to any of her current work. She reached for her letter opener and then removed the single sheet of paper from the envelope.

Ms. Alaina LeBeau,

I am writing to inform you of the death of your stepfather, Trenton Purcell. He passed away one month ago after a long-term illness. While Mr. Purcell had controlling interest of your mother's property during his lifetime, the will left by your mother indicated that all her property was to transfer to her three daughters, with a single stipulation: each of you must occupy the property for a minimum of two consecutive weeks.

I have tried to find a way around this stipulation, as most individuals cannot take a two-week break from their normal lives to live in another town, but

the wording is unshakable. I am afraid that in order
to inherit, all of you must fulfill the terms of the
will or the property will be auctioned off and the
proceeds passed to secondary heirs and charities.

You do not have to occupy the property at the
same time, but each of you must take residence in
the year following the death of your stepfather. That
gives you each eleven months to meet the terms of
the will. Please give me a call at your earliest convenience so that we can discuss your availability to
fulfill these terms.
Sincerely,
William Harold Duhon,
Attorney at Law

She stared at the letter for several seconds, then
dropped it on the desk as if it were going to burn her fingers. All these years she'd assumed her mother had left it
all to that worthless man she'd married. Over the years,
she'd written letters to Purcell, begging him for information on the whereabouts of her sisters, but they'd all
gone unanswered. Every weekend, she'd started to get
into her car and drive to Calais and force him to answer
for what he'd done. Force him to give her the information she wanted. But every time, something stopped her.

She'd known Purcell was still alive when she'd moved
back to Louisiana—had checked enough to know he was
living as a recluse, with almost no contact with the outside world. She'd assumed that the home she'd been born
in and spent the first seven years of her life was lost to
her forever, along with the sisters she had to struggle to
remember.

And now, it was all being offered to her for a mere
fourteen days out of her life. Considering she'd just in-

definitely cleared her schedule, it didn't seem a bad proposition. She had no idea what state the house and grounds were in, but at one time, it had been a beautiful estate. More important, the tiny bayou village of Calais was the perfect place to close herself off from society and figure out what she wanted to do with her life. She'd have all the time in the world to contemplate her options, tucked away deep in the swamp with only the mosquitoes to bother her.

And her mother's ghost.

Chapter Two

Carter Trahan tossed the paper onto his mother's kitchen table. "This is crap," he said.

"Carter Frederic Trahan!" His mother glared at him as she placed cups of coffee on the table in front of him and William Duhon.

"No, no, that's quite all right," said the silver-haired gentleman, who had been a longtime friend of his mother's. "The entire situation is a bit unorthodox."

"It's—" he glanced over at his mother, who was frowning at him from the adjacent chair "—worse than unorthodox. It can't possibly even be legal."

"Oh, I assure you that the terms of the will, while a bit unusual, are completely legal."

"I meant the other part," Carter said. "The part where the sheriff has to play babysitter to fulfill the terms of this will. You can't make me do something that's not in my job description."

William sighed. "You're right on that part. A promise made over fifty years ago can hardly be legally imposed on the current sheriff. But in the spirit of the agreement, I was hoping you'd help out an old friend."

Carter looked across the table at the man who'd been his mother's biggest supporter when his father had been killed, and sighed. "That was low," he muttered.

William beamed. "So you'll do it?"

"Explain it to me again."

"Each sister must occupy the house for two weeks in a row within the next eleven months. If they are outside of the estate borders for more than twenty-four hours, then the fourteen-day timetable starts all over."

"And they've all agreed to come?"

"Not exactly."

"What do you mean 'not exactly'? I thought they all had to do it or the deal was off."

"Thus far, I've been able to locate only one of the sisters, but she's agreed to the terms despite the fact that it could all come to nothing if her sisters aren't located."

Carter frowned. "Why doesn't she know where her sisters are?"

"Because that evil man sent those girls away after their mother died." Carter's mother broke into the conversation.

Carter stared. His mother was not one to throw around words like *evil* in a cavalier manner.

"Don't give me that look," she said. "That greedy no-count married their mother for her money and he killed her by breaking her heart. Her body wasn't even cold before he shipped those girls off to anyone who would take them."

A flash of anger rushed through Carter. "But no one would take all three?"

William shook his head, his expression sad. "If Ophelia had taken the proper steps before she died, things could have turned out differently for the girls. But as it stood, Trenton Purcell had legal control over her assets until his death. The life estate she created right after they married was still in effect."

"The girls weren't his," Carter's mother said, "so he felt they weren't his responsibility."

Carter shook his head. "In the interest of manners, I'm not going to say it," he said to his mother, "but you know what I'm thinking."

His mother nodded. "On this, we're in complete agreement."

"Okay," Carter said, "so when you locate the other two sisters, you'll get them to coordinate a date?"

"Actually, the girls don't have to occupy the property at the same time. As they are adults with lives already in place, they will start occupation at a time that's convenient for them. Assuming, of course, that abandoning your life and moving to the swamp for two weeks is ever convenient."

Carter felt some of the wind come out of his sails. "You mean I might have to do this three times?"

"I'm afraid so."

Carter looked over at the expectant expression on his mother's face. Even though every fiber of his body screamed at him to sprint away from this convoluted family mess, the reality was his mother rarely asked him for anything, and doing this would make her happy.

"Fine. Has the located sister set a date yet?"

"She's the oldest and, as a matter of fact, was available to come immediately."

"Not much of a life if she can drop everything in a matter of days," Carter mumbled.

His mother swatted him with her napkin.

"She's not wanted for anything, is she?" Carter asked.

"Carter!" His mother stared at him in dismay.

William chuckled. "Nothing of the sort. She'd just resigned her position as an attorney and wants to use the time to contemplate the direction she wishes to take her career."

"An attorney. Great."

"Oh, she's quite good. Went to work for one of the best firms in Baton Rouge after graduating top of her class at Boston College."

"A lawyer *and* a Yankee—the hits just keep on coming."

His mother sighed. "Alaina was probably seven years old before she was shipped off to a distant cousin in New England. I expect she hasn't forgotten everything about Southern living or she wouldn't have moved back after getting her education. It's not like she has other family here."

"She's about the same age as me, right?" Carter asked. "How come I don't remember her?"

"Ophelia didn't allow her to attend school with other kids. She claimed homeschooling was the best education, but I often wondered if that was Trenton's idea and not hers. She was a social woman before Trenton came along. But after their marriage, you almost never saw her out in Calais."

Carter frowned. The entire situation stank to high heaven. "What I don't get is, how come none of them came back before now?"

William shrugged. "I can't answer for the girls. I'm sure they all had their reasons, but I am certain none of them knew about the stipulations in their mother's will. This inheritance is completely unexpected, so I would hazard a guess that they felt they had no reason to return."

"So all I have to do is check in every day and make sure they're still on the estate, right?"

"That's it. I'll leave the scheduling to you, but I've made Alaina aware that she needs to work around your job."

"And she had no problem with that?"

"She's an attorney. She has a lot of respect for law enforcement."

"Then she's not like the attorneys I've known—present company excluded, of course."

"I appreciate your handling this for me." William rose from the table, wisely deciding not to overstay his welcome. Carter's mother followed him to the front door where he gave her a kiss on the cheek.

"Call me if you need anything," William said.

"Of course," his mother said. "And don't worry, I'll see that Carter doesn't scare the woman away from her inheritance."

His mother closed the door, then came back into the kitchen and sat down again, frowning.

"I don't like it," Carter said.

"I don't either, but not for the same reasons."

"What about it bothers you?"

She gazed out the back window and shook her head. "I can't put my finger on it. I never liked Trenton Purcell. I always got a bad feeling in his presence. After he and Ophelia married, they pretty much disappeared from society, and I don't think he left the house even once after Ophelia's death. He didn't even attend her funeral."

"Sounds like a stellar guy."

His mother nodded. "No one liked him, but until then, we had nothing concrete to point at and say, 'He's completely wrong.'"

"But?" Carter was certain she hadn't finished her thoughts on Purcell, and he knew his mother well enough to know that her "feelings" about things were not something he should ignore. He didn't know what made her so intuitive, but she'd been right so many times about seemingly straightforward things that weren't straightforward at all that he'd started paying attention when she got the least bit uneasy.

"*But* something about all of this doesn't add up for me." She held up a hand to stop him before he could speak. "I don't think William sees anything unusual except for the legal arrangement itself, which is apparently aboveboard, so don't go thinking he's keeping something from us."

"It bothers me," Carter agreed, "and I didn't even know the man, except by rare sighting when we sneaked onto the property as kids. But if he married the woman for her money, then abandoned her kids when she died, I expect you wouldn't get a good feeling about him."

"Certainly not, but it's more than that." She reached over to place her hand on top of his. "Promise me you'll be careful. Be more watchful than usual. That you won't dismiss anything to do with that house or the girls as simple oddity or coincidence."

He frowned. His mother's concern for him and others was nothing new. She was a wonderful woman with a huge heart. The concern didn't bother him at all.

But the fear in her voice did.

ALAINA TURNED HER SUV onto a narrow dirt road that seemed to lead directly into the swamp. The cypress trees were so thick overhead that they almost formed a canopy over the road, the moss clinging to the limbs blocking everything but the stray ray of sunshine from creeping through.

Her right front wheel sank into a huge dip and she pressed the gas to push the vehicle out of the hole. *It's a good thing I didn't go for the convertible sports car.* She wouldn't have given a low-profile car a hundred yards on this road before it left the driver stranded.

She glanced down at the directions she'd received from

the attorney, to double-check the accuracy, but she already knew she was on the right road. Details were her specialty and the attorney had given very descriptive instructions. She just needed to come to grips with the fact that it looked as if she was driving into the abyss.

She'd just turned seven years old when her mother passed and she'd gone to live with a distant cousin in Boston. The woman and her husband hadn't been well-off, but they'd loved her and cared for her as they had their own son and daughter. But despite the fact that they'd all made her feel welcome and loved, she'd never felt as though Boston was home, not even when she was living in the college dorms.

All those years, it was as if Louisiana called to her, beckoning her to return home. She hadn't taken that call to be literal, because she'd thought her childhood home to be something forever lost to her; and she had no interest at all in seeking out the man who'd treated her mother horribly, then split up her children, sending them to the far ends of the country to become someone else's responsibility.

She'd thought going away to college would eliminate the draw. Once she was around like-minded peers and out of the environment where she was odd man out, she'd hoped she'd finally feel as if she belonged. But despite her contentment with school and a close group of friends, mental images of the swamp haunted her subconscious, finding their way into her dreams.

Her conscious mind wasn't as clear on the details, so the dark patch of dirt now passing as a road didn't appear familiar. She wondered if the house would.

It felt like an eternity that she inched her SUV down the makeshift trail. But finally, after easing her way around a sharp turn in the road, the house came into view, looming above her.

Involuntarily, she hit the brakes and stared, sucking in a breath. On a conscious level, it was as if she was seeing it for the first time. The dreary stone facade and sharp peaks of the roof didn't register mentally, but her body responded. Her chest tightened and her pulse increased.

It scared her.

The thought ripped through her mind and she immediately chided herself. *You've spent your entire life focused on the facts and what you could prove. Now you're letting yourself lose it with fanciful thoughts. Get a grip.*

She closed her eyes, took a deep breath and slowly blew it out. Then she opened her eyes and studied the house with the critical eye she used to study witnesses in a courtroom.

It was still gloomy with its broken shutters and paint peeling on the wooden eaves. The lawn—if one could even call it that—had been swallowed up by weeds and swamp grass that stood at least a foot high. Even the flower beds had been overrun, the stone edging barely visible behind the foliage. An enormous marble fountain that stood in the center of the circular drive had probably been beautiful at one time; but now it was covered with vines, its base filled with murky, stagnant water.

The attorney who'd explained the terms of the inheritance had called the estate "serviceable, if not pleasant." Alaina decided he must be very good at his job. Legally, she couldn't fault his description, but it left out so much.

It's only two weeks.

Mr. Duhon had assured her that any repairs necessary to habitation would be handled by his firm, so it was merely a matter of picking up the phone if she found anything unlivable. A caretaker lived in a cottage somewhere on the property, but the attorney had warned her that the man was elderly and had not been allowed to hire help to keep up the property.

The results of yet another poor decision made by her stepfather spread out before her.

She pulled her SUV around the circular drive that had more weeds showing than the paved stones that comprised it, and parked as close as she could to the front doors. Dark clouds swirled overhead, and she worried that the storm that was scheduled to move in tonight might make an early appearance.

She'd packed only a single suitcase of personal items, but her laptop and food and living supplies took up another couple of boxes. With any luck, she'd get it all inside before the dam broke. Her suitcase had wheels, so she rolled it up the walkway and dragged it up the stone steps to the front door. She removed the enormous iron key from her purse and slid it into the lock, wondering if it would work in the rusted lock.

To her surprise, it turned easily, and a loud click echoed in the silent courtyard. She pushed the ten-foot wooden door open and stepped inside.

The entry resembled a museum more than a home. A huge, round open area stretched up two stories, a giant spiral staircase offering passage from the first floor to the balcony that circled above. Rooms and hallways branched off from the open area in every direction on both floors. Marble columns stood randomly throughout the downstairs area, vases and statues covered with thick layers of dust perching on top of them.

Okay, definitely kind of creepy.

That was her official legal opinion and the best prosecutor in the world couldn't talk her out of it. Still, creepy was tolerable, especially with strong overhead lights. She reached for the switch plate behind her and the area surrounding the front door flooded with light.

She peered into the dim center of the enormous entry and frowned. Surely there was more lighting than this. Checking the wall behind her, she noticed another switch, this one lower on the wall than the light switch she'd flipped earlier. She reached over and pushed the remaining switch up.

The load groan and high-pitched squeals of machinery startled her and she stifled a scream as she scanned the room for the source of the noise. A sheet of light hit the floor in the entry and she looked up to see the roof sliding open. The flickering sun glinted off the glass ceiling the sliding panel exposed inch by inch. From the sounds of metal grinding, the panels hadn't been opened in some time.

Saying a silent prayer that they didn't break and cause the whole thing to come crashing down into the house, she watched until the panels slid completely from view. Relieved that she hadn't broken anything after barely getting in the door, she took her first good look at the giant entry.

She sighed. It certainly didn't look more cheerful in the light, and the cleanliness factor had actually dropped several points, but it gave her something to do. Manual labor was her preferred method of freeing her mind for thought. This house would provide plenty of thinking projects. And maybe, at the end of her two weeks, she'd have a plan for her career, for her life. Heck, fourteen days of cleaning this place and she might solve world hunger.

She hurried back to her SUV to get the rest of her supplies. Once she had everything inside, she'd go exploring for the necessities—kitchen, bathroom, bedroom and laundry facilities. Mr. Duhon had assured her all the necessary items were functional, so at least she didn't have to worry about scrubbing her underwear on a stone in the fountain or cooking dinner over an open fire in the courtyard.

Twenty minutes later, she had a pile of boxes and bags just inside the front door and felt less than excited about lugging them farther. The years of college study and sitting at a desk all day had apparently outweighed her morning jogs, especially when added on top of a long, somewhat apprehensive drive.

She glanced around the entry, figuring she'd find the kitchen first, then finally set off down a wide hallway to her left, assuming the largest hallways were more likely to lead to well-used areas. At the end of the hallway, a large arch opened into a spacious kitchen and breakfast area.

The room was at least twenty-five feet square with miles of stone countertops and windows framing every wall of the eating area. She looked out at the weeds and vines and froze as a sudden flash of pink azaleas, lush grass and a blooming magnolia tree ran through her mind. She'd eaten here looking out into the onetime beautiful gardens. It was so clear in her mind that it was as if she were looking at a snapshot.

Sighing, she walked back down the hall to begin moving the supplies to the kitchen. What had just happened was something she needed to get used to. She'd been old enough to remember the house when she'd left, but the trauma of losing her mother and her sisters all at once had forced those memories so far back into the recesses of her mind that she wondered if they'd been gone forever. Apparently that wasn't the case; and being in the house was probably going to bring back some of those memories.

Maybe that was a good thing. At seven years old, she hadn't been capable of processing what she'd been through on a logical level. Now that she was an adult, maybe it was time she dealt with her less-than-stellar past once and for all. Maybe it was something she needed to do to move forward with her career and her personal life.

The only clear memory she had was of that night—the night before they were sent away. And the sheer figure of her mother, dressed in a long white flowing gown and hovering over her bed.

She shook her head, trying to clear the image from her mind. It had been frozen there for so long, the lone thing she'd carried with her all these years. Logically, she knew that she'd been a scared little girl who'd just lost her mother, but emotionally, she still wondered if what she'd seen that night was real.

As she stepped back into the entry, she heard a noise overhead. Immediately she froze, trying to determine if she'd heard the normal sounds of an old house, or if something else, of the four-legged, undesirable variety, was inside with her. Her pulse quickened when she realized it was footsteps—the two-legged kind.

A single glance at the crack in the front door made her blood run cold. She was positive she'd closed and locked it behind her after carrying in the last of the supplies. But someone was inside with her.

She reached for her purse and pulled out the pistol she'd begun carrying after receiving her first official death threat on the job. Despite the heat and humidity, the metal was cold in her hand. She dug around in the side pocket for her car keys and mentally cursed when she remembered she'd set them on the kitchen counter.

She eased back down the hallway, praying she could get her keys and get out of the house. Surely someone with a legitimate reason to be inside would have knocked or called out upon entering. She could only assume that whoever had come in was up to no good. That was a problem for the sheriff, not an unemployed attorney who had no interest in playing the hero.

The footsteps faded away as she slipped down the hallway and into the kitchen to retrieve her car keys. She moved silently on the stone floor, giving mental thanks that she'd worn comfortable tennis shoes and jeans and not her usual casual wear of slacks, blouse and high-heeled sandals.

All she had to do was make it back down the hallway and out of the house. An athletic scholarship for sprinting had paid for most of her college. If she could get outside the house, she had no doubt she could beat the intruder to her SUV and get away. But as she hurried across the kitchen to the hallway, the pantry door flew open. Unable to stop, she collided with it and went sprawling to the ground, her pistol sliding across the stone floor.

She scrambled for the gun as a dark figure stepped out of the pantry. Panicked, she made a desperate reach for the pistol, which was still several inches away.

"I wouldn't do that if I were you." A deep voice sounded above her.

Chapter Three

One look at the man and she knew she didn't stand a chance. He was easily six feet tall, with strong arms and chest. The butt of a pistol peeked out of the waistband of his jeans and she had no doubt he could fire before she could even latch on to her weapon.

This was it. Her life would come full circle in this swamp—birth to death.

"Alaina LeBeau?" he asked, staring down at her with a mixture of aggravation and resignation.

"Yes." She pushed herself up to a sitting position.

He studied her face for a moment, then sighed and extended his hand to help her up from the floor. "I didn't mean to scare you."

"Then why were you sneaking around my house and hiding in the pantry?" The fear she'd felt only seconds ago was speeding away, only to be replaced by aggravation now that she no longer felt threatened.

His green eyes flashed with anger. "I don't 'sneak around' private property, and that's not a pantry—it's a stairwell."

She peered around him into the doorway and, sure enough, saw a narrow set of stairs leading up to the second floor. "Who are you and what are you doing here?"

"I'm Carter Trahan—Sheriff Carter Trahan—and I'm here to check off one day on my babysitting roster."

Alaina clenched her jaw, forcing herself to pause before replying to his insulting statement. The last thing she needed was to alienate the man required to check up on her. "Mr. Duhon informed me that you'd be *monitoring* the residency terms of the will. I hardly need a babysitter."

He merely raised one eyebrow and gave her an amused smile.

"Well, if you're done slamming doors into visitors, Sheriff Trahan, I should get back to my unpacking. Next time you check on me, please knock."

"I did knock…twice. Then I opened the door and called out from the entrance. I thought my voice would echo up to the second floor, but you kept on walking, so I went upstairs to catch you there."

Alaina stared at him. "That's impossible. I haven't been upstairs yet."

Carter frowned. "I saw someone enter the hallway upstairs that runs parallel to this one."

Her breath caught in her throat. "It wasn't me," she managed, "and I came here alone. Perhaps the caretaker…"

He shook his head. "Amos is eighty-six years old and walks with a limp. Whoever this was walked quickly enough to disappear before I got upstairs. When I got to the bedroom over the kitchen, I could hear noise downstairs. The door to the servant's stairwell was partially open, so I assumed you'd gone down that way."

He pushed shut the door to the stairwell and had to give it an extra nudge when it jammed in the doorframe. "The door had no lock, but it stuck when I tried to open it. I hit it with my shoulder, which is why it flew open and struck you. But if anyone had used it right before me, you would have heard and seen them."

"I heard *you* walking upstairs. That's why I was hurrying to get out of the house, but I didn't hear anyone before."

Alaina crossed her arms in front of her chest, a slight chill running over her. "You're sure you saw someone? Maybe it was a trick of shadows and light. Between the storm brewing and that glass ceiling, maybe it just looked like someone was upstairs."

"Maybe," he said, but he didn't look as though he believed it for a minute.

He spun around and strode down the hallway to the entry. Ignoring his abrupt departure, Alaina hurried behind him as he knelt in front of the circular stairs.

"Only one set of prints, and they're mine," he said, pointing to the prints that led up the dusty staircase.

"Maybe it was a ghost," Alaina joked.

Carter rose and narrowed his eyes at her. "What ghost?"

She shrugged. "None in particular. I just figured old, spooky house equaled a ghost story of some sort, especially in a small community."

"The locals have their share of beliefs about this house and your stepfather, but I prefer to deal with what I can prove. Given your profession, I assume you appreciate that."

"Of course. I was just joking." But she knew she was lying, before the words left her mouth. The memory of her mother's ghost was something she couldn't deny and had never been able to forget.

"Because I don't believe in ghosts," he said, "I'm going to take a look around."

"Of course… Thank you."

He nodded. "Do you know how to use that pistol?"

"Yes. I practice at the range at least once a week."

"Keep it on you. I'll make sure I announce myself before accosting you again."

He pulled his pistol from his waistband and strode up the stairs. She watched him for a couple of seconds, then ran back to the kitchen to scoop her pistol up from the floor. Her apprehension when she'd first arrived had turned into full-fledged worry.

Something didn't feel right.

The last time she'd felt that way, a child had died.

CARTER PEERED INTO each bedroom off the main hallway over the kitchen, but none of them showed any signs of human passage. Tiny tracks of four-legged critters appeared periodically, but he easily identified and dismissed them. Four-legged creatures may not be desirable inside a home, but there were worse things.

The more space he covered with no indication of the intruder, the more frustrated he became with the entire situation. When William had described Alaina as a successful Baton Rouge attorney, Carter had immediately formed a mental picture of a masculine-looking female. The tall, fit woman with hazel eyes and miles of wavy brown hair didn't fit into his image at all.

He'd expected to be annoyed and he was, but he hadn't expected to find her attractive, and that annoyed him even more.

Peering into the last bedroom along the hallway, he blew out a breath. There was no indication that anyone had traveled down this hall besides him, but he knew he'd seen something. Or maybe Alaina was right and the weather and glass ceiling had conspired to create a shadow he had taken for a person.

He started around the balcony that circled the entry, checking the rooms that shot off in every direction. None of them appeared disturbed until he reached the last. *Trenton Purcell's office,* he thought as he stepped inside. A huge ornate desk stood in the center of the room. Bookcases, stuffed with leather-bound texts, formed every square inch of the walls, even framing the doorway.

The layer of dust here wasn't as thick as it was in the rest of the rooms, which made sense assuming Purcell had spent a lot of time in here. He took a step toward the desk and realized that a narrow doorway sat in the back corner of the room, barely visible because it was stained the same color as the bookcases.

He pushed the door open to find a bedroom with another entry off the balcony. The bed was still covered with navy sheets and spread, and several bottles of medicine stood on the nightstand. He picked one up and checked to make sure it belonged to Purcell, then placed it back on the table.

Three doors occupied the far wall of the bedroom, one standing open, exposing the master bath. He opened the second door and found a musty walk-in closet, still full of tattered suits. He expected the third door was more storage but found another servant's staircase instead.

It made sense, he supposed, that the servants would have a private entry into the master bedroom. That way, they couldn't be seen going about their work by any household guests. At least, it made sense as much as having people living in your home and waiting on you did to Carter. He wasn't convinced the convenience was worth the loss of privacy.

He followed the staircase down and pushed open the door at the bottom. It opened easily and without a sound and he stepped out into a laundry room at the back of the house. A door leading into the backyard was positioned at the rear of the room. A quick check showed it to be locked, but he pulled it open and studied the ground outside, trying to make out footprints. Unfortunately, ground cover of cracked stones, dirt and vines wasn't the kind of material that was easily imprinted.

He stepped back inside and closed and locked the door. There was absolutely no indication that anyone had been in the house except him and Alaina. The fact that he'd found nothing to suggest the presence of an intruder should make him happy, but he couldn't work himself up to that point.

The reality was, for the first time in his life, Carter knew exactly what his mother meant when she said she "felt" something was wrong but couldn't put her finger on it. Something was very wrong in this house.

Whatever it was, he didn't think it would remain hidden for long.

Chapter Four

Alaina felt as though she'd waited forever, but finally Carter emerged from one of the back hallways and into the massive entry room. She let out a breath she hadn't realized she was holding and felt the tightness in her chest release. Then she realized that he'd just entered the room from the first floor but hadn't used either of the stairwells to get down from the second floor.

"How did you get downstairs?" she asked as he approached.

He frowned. "A servant's stairwell in the master bedroom. It led to the laundry room off the back of the house."

"How many hidden passages are in this house?"

"More than I've found so far, I'd guess." He didn't look happy about it.

"Did you see anyone…? I mean, I guess you didn't, but did you see any sign that someone had been up there?"

"No."

"But?"

He sighed. "But I don't believe in fanciful things like ghosts and I have perfect vision. I saw something on that landing."

"An animal maybe?"

"It was too large to be any animal that would be in the house and I couldn't find tracks on the landing."

She swallowed. "Then maybe it was a shadow. With that enormous glass ceiling and the storm brewing, couldn't it have created a moving shadow that looked like a person?"

"I suppose," he said, but didn't seem convinced. "Look, maybe you shouldn't stay here just yet."

His suggestion was tempting, especially given that she was completely creeped out, but it wasn't conducive to the reason she was there.

"Is there a hotel in town?" she asked, wondering if spending the night in a hotel and milling among the locals the rest of the day would give whoever was lurking in the house the notice to clear out—assuming it was a human in the first place. Rats, raccoons and storm clouds probably wouldn't care about the local gossip.

"No hotel. No rental property either. Calais is a small spot on the map and a dead end at that. People don't come here unless they intend to, so there's not much call for hotels and such. New Orleans is only a little over an hour's drive, though." He looked hopeful as he delivered that last statement.

She could do it—probably should do it—but the thought of packing everything back in her SUV and spending another hour plus on the road didn't sound even remotely appealing. If she thought it would change something, she might consider it, but staying in New Orleans wouldn't create any local gossip at all. It would only be delaying the inevitable.

She sighed. "I appreciate your concern, but if you saw something tangible, my staying in New Orleans for a night isn't going to make it clear out. And it's just one more day I'll have to make up staying here."

"It would give me a chance to poke around some more."

"You're welcome to do that while I'm here. In fact, as

I'll be the one living here for two weeks, I'd prefer it if I did it with you."

She could tell by the way his jaw flexed that he didn't like it. The attorney had already warned her that the sheriff who'd agreed to the terms of the will had long since passed. While the new sheriff had agreed to meet the terms of the will, he was neither under any legal obligation to do so, nor was he being paid for his time.

His babysitting comment earlier had left her no doubt as to how he felt about his assignment. She sympathized with his position, but ultimately it wasn't her problem. If he didn't want to deal with it any longer, Alaina was certain Mr. Duhon would find someone else.

Finally, he blew out a breath. "Okay, then the first thing we should do is locate a bedroom for you that is easily secured. No servants' passages and a good, sturdy lock."

"One with a connecting bath would be best."

"I agree. The master bedroom has a connecting bath but also several ways in and out."

She crossed her arms over her chest, as if to ward off the unease she felt at the thought of sleeping in the same bed that her dead stepfather had slept in. "I wouldn't want to sleep in there anyway."

"I don't blame you. Let's check downstairs first."

Alaina nodded and walked to the left side of the entry as Carter took the right. A careful inspection of the downstairs rooms did not reveal any equipped as a bedroom.

"We could move some bedroom furniture downstairs," Carter suggested as they met at the back of the entry.

She shook her head. "There's no connecting bath for any of the rooms. There's a half bath off the kitchen, but that's the only one I've seen downstairs so far."

"There's another off the laundry room."

She blew out a breath. "Both of those are hallways

away from these rooms, and I can hardly put a bed in the middle of the kitchen or the laundry room, or shower in the sink."

"No. Neither of those rooms is secure anyway. They both have wide entries with no doors."

"Probably to make carrying laundry and food easier."

"Which doesn't help us at all."

"Then I guess I'll have to stay upstairs."

He motioned toward the spiral stairwell. "After you."

As she walked up the stairs, she looked out the glass ceiling. The clouds overhead swirled, creating constantly shifting patterns of light and shadows.

"That storm looks like it's going to be bad," she said as they stepped onto the landing.

"It doesn't look like a mild one," he agreed. "I can't believe that glass ceiling is still intact. We had a horrible storm last week—lots of lightning and hail even."

"It's got a panel that covers it. I accidentally opened it thinking it was a switch for the lights. It didn't sound like it had been used in some time."

Carter looked up and frowned. "Your stepfather was a recluse. Maybe he didn't like the light either."

Preferring to lurk in the shadow like most monsters.

She shook her head. Now was not the time for fanciful thoughts, especially those that might scare her once she was alone in this house in the dark. She had no concrete memory of her stepfather, but she knew she'd feared him. That was all she wanted to know.

"I just hope it closes," she said.

"Let's not borrow trouble," he said and pointed to a hallway on the left side of the landing. "I saw several bedrooms that direction when I was up here earlier. Let's see if one works."

By unspoken agreement, they each took a side of the

hall and began inspecting the bedrooms. Alaina made it to the door centered at the end of the hall before Carter. She stepped inside and sucked in a breath.

This was it. The bedroom she'd shared with her sisters.

It was situated directly over the kitchen area and just as large. Her memories were fuzzy, but she could remember the single beds and crib, all decked out in pink and white. White dressers stood against the wall across from the beds. The beds and dressers were long gone, but against the far wall stood two wooden school desks.

She crossed the room and ran her fingers over the dusty desktop. A chill coursed through her when she felt the indentations in the corner. It had been restained and lacquered when she was a child—her punishment had been scrubbing the marble floors downstairs for a week by hand—but even the new stain and lacquer hadn't erased the single word she'd carved in the corner with her scissors.

Help.

"Is everything okay?" Carter's voice sounded behind her, causing her to spin around.

"Sorry," he said. "I didn't mean to startle you." He studied her for a couple of seconds. "Is something wrong?"

"No," she said, straining to keep herself from sounding as anxious as she felt. "Just coming face-to-face with old ghosts."

She forced a small smile. "I suppose I should get used to it, right?"

He looked around the room and she had no doubt he noticed the desks and other remnants that marked the room as occupied by children. "I guess it's strange coming back here after so long. You must have a lot of memories of this place."

"Not really. To be honest, I barely remember anything

about my childhood. I should because I was old enough to, but it's as if it's been erased."

"Perhaps it was too painful to deal with, so you locked away those memories."

A bit of relief washed over her. "Yes, I think you're right. You're very intuitive."

"Not really," he said, looking slightly uncomfortable. "It just seems logical given the circumstances back then."

She studied him for a moment. It was the first time since she'd met him that she got the feeling he was lying to her. As an attorney, she had a highly honed ability to detect untruth.

"Looks like the dam is breaking. I guess that's something else I'll have to deal with," she said, pushing all thought of Carter and his potential ulterior motives from her mind. Whatever Carter was hiding was none of her business. She barely knew the man and that was the way things were going to stay.

He nodded and scanned the room again. "It looks like this is the only one with serviceable furniture, but if you don't feel comfortable staying in here…"

"No, this will be fine."

"Are you sure?"

"It doesn't require moving furniture and is as secure as any other option, right?"

"Assuming the locks work properly, yes." He walked to the doorway and checked the lock, then crossed the room to open the French doors that led onto a balcony overlooking the backyard.

She stepped out to join him. The square lines of cypress trees were the only indicators of the lawn that used to exist. Now it was as if the entire area had been swallowed up by the swamp that surrounded it. Marsh grass and weeds grew as high as a person, and scraggly shrubs had spouted up in random patterns. Vines clung to everything capable of supporting their weight and when nothing was available, they ran across the ground, mixing in with the moss to make a mottled carpet of green.

"It's not very inviting," she said, trying to shake the uneasy feeling that the swamp gave her.

She'd expected Carter to provide another logical explanation—one that she could lock on to and carry over the next two weeks—but instead, he stared silently out across the tangle of undergrowth. Finally, he spoke. "The swamps of Mystere Parish aren't like other places, not even like other swamps."

"What do you mean?"

He shook his head. "Can't say exactly. It's just a feeling, really, that something isn't right. Swamps in Mystere Parish are quieter than most and have more than their share of unexplained phenomena."

"The legends and lore of Creoles?"

"I'm sure that's some of it, but I'm not much for old wives' tales or stories told to scare kids into minding their mothers. Still, I don't much like spending time in the swamp." He looked her straight in the eyes. "I'm not trying to tell you what to do, but you probably shouldn't venture out there. Too many lethal things could be lurking just past your back door and not a single one of them the kind of thing legends are made from."

Despite the heat of the evening, a slight chill ran over her and she crossed her arms. "You don't have to worry about that for a second. You couldn't pay me enough to go in there."

He nodded. "Well, the locks on both doors are fine. I wish we could have found a room closer to the stairwell…"

His voice trailed off and Alaina realized he hadn't

wanted to alarm her by finishing his sentence, but she had little doubt what he was thinking.

"In case I need to get out in a hurry," she finished for him.

He frowned. "I don't want to scare you unnecessarily, but I'd be lying if I said I liked you staying out here alone."

"I thought there was a caretaker."

"Amos lives in his own cabin." He pointed across what used to be the back lawn. "It's somewhere in that mess. Even if he heard or saw anything from his cabin, age and physical conditioning are working against him. He wouldn't be much help."

She leaned over the balcony and was relieved to see a stone walkway below that led around to the front of the house. It was a bit overgrown with vines but still visible.

"No worries," she said as she straightened back up. "If things get hairy, I'll go right over the balcony and run for my SUV."

Carter glanced over the balcony and raised his eyebrows. "You're going to jump from the second floor then run?"

"I went to college on a track-and-field scholarship. Almost made the Olympic team. The drop from the railing is no worse than the high jump, and trust me, if it's a footrace with anything on two legs, I can take them."

His lips quivered for a moment, then broke into a slow smile. "That's good to know, but if it's all the same, I'm going to hope you don't have to back up those words."

She smiled. "Me, too, but if it's all the same, I may sleep with tennis shoes on."

"Well, then, it looks like we have a plan." He stepped back toward the door to the bedroom and motioned her inside. He stood just outside the doorway, waiting for her to pass. As she stepped past him, her arm brushed across his chest and she felt a tingle deep inside. Even though it had been a tiny bit of contact, it had left no doubt that underneath the worn T-shirt and jeans contained a ripped body built for action.

Maybe she needed to revise her earlier statement. She might not be able to take Carter in a footrace, but then, depending on the reason he was chasing her, she might not run.

She shook her head to clear it from thoughts that had no business being there. Had it really been that long since she'd enjoyed the company of a man that she was fantasizing about the first eligible one she ran across? She'd ended a three-year relationship eight months before and hadn't been interested in pursuing another. Or maybe her last relationship had left her so jaded about men—particularly good-looking ones—that she had been intentionally avoiding them.

Funny how she'd managed to do just that in Baton Rouge, the capital of the state, but the second she set foot in a town with less population than her condominium complex, she came face-to-face with the only man who had piqued her interest since her ex.

Carter closed and locked the French doors behind them. "Let me help you get your things up here."

"Oh, that's okay. I brought only one suitcase of personal things. The rest goes to the kitchen. It will give me something to do." She hoped he'd leave her to it. With her imagination in overdrive and her memory rapid-firing without warning and her obvious attraction to the sheriff, she felt too vulnerable. And she didn't like that feeling.

Carter nodded and they made their way back downstairs. He stood in the entryway next to the front door and scanned the area one last time. She could tell he was still uncomfortable with her staying here alone—and that made two of them—but she wasn't about to admit it. The sooner she got started, the sooner her fourteen-day stint would be over. Besides, she couldn't put her career on hold forever. A delay meeting the terms of the will would delay anything else she decided, as well.

"Can I see your cell phone?" Carter asked.

"What? Oh, sure." She dug the phone out of her purse and handed it to him.

He checked the display and frowned. "Only one bar. I figured as much. When the storm hits, you may lose service altogether."

He pressed the phone's screen for a minute, then handed it back to her. "I loaded my cell number in favorites along with the number for dispatch. As soon as you get a chance, you should head to the café—they have free Wi-Fi—and download that app that allows you to put a phone number on your screen for speed dial."

She stared at him for a moment.

"I'm not trying to scare you," he said. "It's just that the house is old and poorly maintained and there are a lot of things that could become an emergency. William Duhon is a family friend, and I promised him I'd look after things. He has an office here in Calais, but also in New Orleans, so he's not always readily available."

She nodded. "That's a good idea. And thank you for being on call."

He handed the phone back to her, but as she was about to pull her hand away, he gently clasped his hand around it. "If you see anything that doesn't look right—hell, if you *feel* like something's not right—call me."

The heat from his hand coursed through her and she suddenly realized how close they were standing to each other. If she tilted her face upward and leaned in just a bit, it was all it would take to kiss him.

She pulled her hand away. "I can hardly bother you with every little noise. I'm sure there are plenty of things here that are going to try my nerves. This isn't exactly the kind of living arrangement I'm used to."

He shook his head. "Don't give me that. If you were any good at being a lawyer, then you know how to read a situation better than most. I'm asking you not to second-guess yourself."

A bit of annoyance started to creep in. Caution was one thing, but now she felt as if he was trying to scare her. And certainly, he had no right making assumptions about her professional abilities. "Look, I appreciate your concern, but other than ensuring I don't leave town, I'm not really your responsibility."

His expression didn't change except for a tiny flex of his jaw. Her words had—what?—annoyed him? Frustrated him? She couldn't tell exactly.

"As long as William Duhon is my mother's best friend, then you're my responsibility. You may as well get used to it."

He opened the front door and left without so much as a backward glance. She watched as he pulled away in his truck and then she shut the door and locked it. Mr. Duhon hadn't told her that a hulking male was part of the deal.

Unlocked memories, ghosts, storms and a creepy house being swallowed up by the swamp. She had to face all of them for thirteen more days.

At the moment, the hunky sheriff was the thing that scared her most of all.

Chapter Five

As he drove away, Carter glanced in his rearview mirror at the decaying old house that seemed to fade into the swamp. This entire situation had gone from annoying to frustrating in very little time. And the worst part was, he had a feeling things were only going to go downhill from here. Darn his mother and her "feelings." Although he'd never really understood what she meant when she said things felt wrong, he'd always respected her perception.

Now he understood it all too well.

Something was wrong—seriously wrong—at that house. Alaina seemed nice enough for a lawyer, and he certainly hadn't missed the fact that she was easy on the eyes, but he got the impression she was hiding something. Granted, she had no call to lay out her life to a complete stranger, and he didn't expect her to, but her safety was in question and it almost seemed as if she was hiding things to do with the house and her childhood there.

A string of curse words ran through his head, but he managed to hold them in, as his mother had taught him to. When he reached the crossroads in Calais, he gave up manners—after all, he was the only one in the vehicle—and let one slip. Then he turned his truck toward William's office. He needed more information and the best place to start was with the attorney handling the estate.

William was just locking up his office on Main Street when Carter parked in front of it. He gave Carter a pleasant smile as the sheriff exited his truck.

"I trust Alaina arrived safely?" William asked.

"She arrived safely, but I have some concerns about her ability to remain that way. Do you have some time to talk?"

"Certainly. Let me open back up."

"Actually," Carter interrupted him before he could unlock the door, "I could really use a cup of coffee and a Danish."

William smiled. "I would never say no to coffee and Danish. The café it is, then."

They walked in silence across the street to Calais Café and slid into a booth in the far corner. Only a couple of tables were occupied, but they were far enough away that they could speak freely without fear of being overheard.

Seconds later, the waitress walked up. "Good evening, gentlemen," she said with a big smile.

"I don't know about the 'gentlemen' part," Carter joked.

"Speak for yourself, young man," William said.

The waitress, a young, pretty girl named Connie, who'd turned up in Calais several months before, laughed at their exchange.

"Trust me," she said, "after working at a dive in New Orleans, I can assure you that the citizens of Calais are above reproach."

Carter smiled at the woman. "Then good evening to you, too."

William nodded. "As well from me."

"Are you having supper," Connie asked, "or are you planning to cheat on supper with a Danish?"

"Given that my supper is most likely microwavable," Carter said, "*cheating* is a strong word."

Connie shook her head. "The quality of the object is not the issue. Once you've committed to something, it's still cheating. But I guess I'll have pity on you. What about you, Mr. Duhon?"

"I'll be cheating as well," William said, "but don't tell Matilda."

Connie laughed as she walked away. William's dedication to his late wife's ancient white Persian was a commonly known fact in Calais.

William glanced at Connie as she walked away, then looked back at Carter. "She's a pretty girl. Seems nice, as well."

Something in William's voice set Carter on high alert and he looked over at the attorney, taking in the slightly hopeful expression on his face. "Oh, no!" Carter said. "Don't you even go there."

"Why, I didn't say a word."

"Uh-huh. You and my mother are always 'never saying a word.' And all those words you're never saying come back to the same thing—when am I going to settle down and give her grandkids."

Connie returned with a tray and placed the coffee and two enormous Danish on the table. "Enjoy," she said and hurried away to greet customers entering the café.

William took a bite of the Danish dripping with cream, and smiled. "Your mother is my oldest and dearest friend. I'd hardly be doing my job if I didn't try to get her the things she wants most in life."

Carter stuffed a huge bite of Danish in his mouth and held up one finger until he managed to wash the pastry down with coffee. "Get her a puppy and tell her to make do. The whole 'kids and white picket fence' thing isn't in my long-term plans."

The attorney sighed. "You're still young. Perhaps you'll

change your mind and your mother can die a fulfilled woman."

"Ha! You're not going to guilt me into shackling myself to some woman either. Look, I know you and my mother both had great marriages and both of you lost spouses way too early, but it's not for everyone. Some people have such a narrow slot for entry that they never find someone who fits it."

"Some people board up that slot so that it is too narrow for others to enter."

"Perhaps, but that's my choice. And besides, even if I had the Grand Canyon of slots, the last thing I'd want is a young, innocent, nice girl. Living with me would be hell on earth to someone like that."

Instantly, his thoughts flashed to Alaina. Now, there was a woman who wouldn't let a man get the better of her. Likely, she'd get the best of any man she tangled with. He shook his head, wondering why he found that remotely attractive. Clearly he had issues. Danger attracted him. Nice, pretty girls with a good sense of humor bored him.

"So who is she?" William asked, breaking him out of his thoughts.

"What? No one."

William wagged a finger at him. "I saw the look on your face. You went someplace where you were thinking about a woman—maybe one thin enough to fit in that slot."

"The woman I was thinking about would blow up the slot with dynamite and stroll through. She's also the reason I need to talk to you."

"You're speaking of Alaina? I haven't seen her since she was a child, of course, but her mother was quite beautiful."

"She's beautiful…and prickly and not much on giving information."

William smiled. "Got under your skin, did she?" He rubbed his jaw a moment. "I suppose with her being an attorney, she'd be naturally cautious, especially with anything she considered personal or outside of the scope of your business with the estate. Is there anything in particular that concerns you?"

"Yeah." He told William about what he'd seen in the house and his failure to find any good explanation.

"And you don't accept that it could have been tricks of light and shadows, as Alaina suggested?"

Carter blew out a breath. "I should. I mean, it's far more logical than someone walking around the house but not leaving a trace in all that dust…."

"But?"

"But I know what I saw and it wasn't a shadow." He paused for a moment, trying to think of how to sum up his assessment in a way that didn't make him sound crazy. "Look, something's not right. I can't put my finger on it, but I'm as certain about it as I was that the Danish would be superb."

William nodded. "I believe you. You are your mother's son after all. I've always figured it was only a matter of time before you tapped into the same perception she has. So what can I do to help?"

"I want information."

"About?"

"We can start with Ophelia LeBeau and Trenton Purcell."

"Okay. What would you like to know?"

"I don't know exactly. Just start talking and maybe it will come to me."

William nodded. "Ophelia was one of the most beautiful women I've ever seen—Alaina looks a lot like her from the pictures I've seen—but it wasn't just the outside. She was beautiful inside, as well. I think perhaps her big heart proved to be her undoing."

"How so?"

"She loved Marcus LeBeau, the girls' father, as deeply and long as the Mississippi River. You could see it all over her face every time she looked at him. And the feeling was mutual. Marcus adored Ophelia and doted on his daughters. When he was killed in a boating accident, I think her heart broke in two."

"Enter Trenton Purcell?"

William nodded. "It's my opinion that Ophelia would never have taken up with him if she hadn't been grieving Marcus's loss. And I also think she wanted the girls to have a father. It was the worst mistake she ever made."

"So I take it you didn't like him either?"

William flushed a bit, his expression slightly angry. "Trenton Purcell was the biggest bastard I've ever come across in all my years on earth. And I trust you won't repeat what I've said to your mother…at least not with those exact words."

"Don't worry. I think you two are in absolute agreement on this one."

"Yes, well, I tried to talk Ophelia out of marrying him—I suggested she live with him rather than making it legally binding. Probably not my kindest moment, but with her own father deceased and my firm managing her estate, I felt responsible." He sighed. "Unfortunately, I wasn't successful—not in convincing her to forgo legally binding herself to him or in trying to get her to address the issues of the estate to protect her daughters."

"I don't get that part. If she loved her children so much, why wouldn't she want them protected?"

William shook his head. "Because she wanted so badly to believe in Purcell and did? Because she was only twenty-eight and couldn't force herself to think about her own death? I can't really say. What I can tell you is that failing to take the legal steps to protect her girls was the second-biggest mistake Ophelia ever made."

"How did Ophelia die?"

"Heart attack was the official ruling, but I'd argue that a more apt description was a broken heart."

"Hmm. Rather a poetic statement for an attorney."

William gave him a small smile. "Comes from having a British mother who loved the classics, I suppose."

"And Purcell? I assume the broken-heart thing wasn't his bag?"

"Hardly, but Purcell had all sorts of issues."

"What do you mean?"

"He was so secretive—people-avoidant, quite frankly. When he moved into the house, he convinced Ophelia to give up all her volunteer work within the community and to pull the girls out of public school. They rarely left the house."

"And after Ophelia died?"

"Until the day the coroner carried his body out, I am not aware that he ever left the house again. The caretaker was born on the estate and never left, so he was on hand to tend to most things day to day, and after Purcell shut himself off, he convinced Jack Granger to play errand boy for him."

"When he was sober enough to drive."

William nodded. "And probably when he wasn't. I think Purcell threw enough money at him to keep him in beer, but not much else. He did some grumbling after Purcell died. I think he was expecting something by way of inheritance."

"So no one knew that Purcell didn't have the authority to dispense Ophelia's money."

"Not unless Purcell told them, and I doubt he would have let that fact loose. I'd hazard a guess that he got cheap labor off some of the Calais citizens for years with promises of riches at his death."

"So there might be some pissed-off people in Calais?"

William shrugged. "Maybe, but Granger is the only one I can think of who still lives here, and anyone with a lick of sense and decency wouldn't begrudge those girls their inheritance, even if it meant that Purcell played them for a fool."

Carter nodded, mulling over everything William had told him. From start to finish to now, it was a strange setup. "The thing I don't understand is, why did Purcell marry Ophelia for her money, then hide away in the bayou after her death? He'd already disposed of her children, so his responsibilities were minimal. Shouldn't he have been on a tropical island with a flock of sexy women?"

"Yes, that would have followed more the norm, but I think that's where Purcell's issues came in. I think he was already pulling away from society and saw Ophelia's riches as a way to avoid any interaction with the outside world because he wouldn't be required to hold a job. Her death only entrenched that belief because without Ophelia and the girls, he had no one pressing him to venture outside of his own mind."

"So he was crazy?"

"I have no medical training for the basis of my opinion, but yes, I'd say crazy. However, crazy, in this case, does not absolve intent. I have no proof, of course, but I think Purcell was a mean man—deliberately mean to Ophelia and the girls. Evil requires calculation."

Carter shook his head, wondering if any of the information he'd gained meant something now. Certainly it gave him a better view of the circumstances that led to his current problem—and gave him at least ten more reasons to hate Purcell—but he wasn't sure it gave him any direction on the situation with Alaina.

He looked over at William. "I don't suppose you believe in ghosts, do you?"

William was silent for a moment. "Well, if it's a ghost you saw, let's hope for Alaina's sake that it was Ophelia and not Trenton."

ALAINA UNPACKED the last of the groceries from the boxes she'd lugged into the kitchen. The staples were strewn across the long stone countertop that formed the bar, but that was all she'd taken the time to wipe down. Tomorrow, she'd lug the boxes with cleaning supplies into the kitchen and tackle the pantry and inside of the cabinets. Once they were clean, she'd head into Calais to get some refrigerated items, now that she'd ensured the ancient appliance was still working.

A burst of thunder fired off and a bolt of lightning flashed across the glass wall of the breakfast area, causing her to jump. The second blast rolled through a couple of seconds later and giant raindrops began to plink against the windows.

The ceiling!

She'd meant to close the roof before she started unpacking but was so distracted that she'd forgotten. She rushed back to the entry and was relieved that no rain poured into the house. Now, as long as the switch worked, she was in business.

Saying a silent prayer, she reached out and flipped the switch. The machinery whined for a couple of seconds, but then the roof started to slide slowly back in place. She blew out a breath of relief as the panel slid over the last foot of the glass.

The lack of light hid the dust and grime, but it invited in the spooky. The vases and other objets d'art that resided on the freestanding columns stood like silent sentinels in the dim light. Surely the entry contained another light source. Glancing down the walls, she spotted sconces placed every twenty feet or so. Now, if she could just find the switch.

She started checking to her right, thinking if it were her house, she'd want a switch located somewhere outside the kitchen, but as she traveled farther and farther away from the kitchen hallway, she realized that logic had apparently not entered into switch-plate placement in this house.

As she drew closer to the back of the entry, in the darkest corner of the room, a buzzer sounded and she barely fought back a scream.

The laundry.

As she headed down the hallway to the laundry room, she chided herself. First the storm; now she was jumping at appliances. Thirteen more days in this house stretched ahead of her. She had to get a grip.

She pulled the sheets from the dryer and transferred the blanket from the washing machine to dry. So far, William's word that the house was serviceable was holding up, which was a relief. She sniffed the sheets and was relieved that the dust and slight smell of mold were no longer present. The last thing she needed was to get sick in this environment. Leaving would be the only way to get healthy again.

As she folded the sheets, lightning flashed, lighting up the overgrown courtyard outside the laundry room. She froze. Was something moving outside? Surely not, given the storm. She placed the sheets on the dryer to try to get a better look.

The humidity from the storm had the glass panels on the door fogging over, thus limiting visibility. She stepped close to the door and rubbed a peephole, then peered out into the darkness. The foliage swayed in the wind, the occasional bursts of lightning casting rays of light in between the branches and leaves. Whatever she'd seen was solid. At least she thought it was, but because she'd caught it out of the corner of her eye, she couldn't be certain.

Her peephole fogged over again and before she could change her mind, she reached for the doorknob. She'd just step out under the overhang and see if she could get a better look.

She sucked in a breath when the knob turned easily in her hand.

It was already unlocked!

She pulled her pistol from her waistband, where she'd stuck it earlier. That door had been locked when she'd started the laundry. She'd checked it herself. As much as she hated to admit it, Carter might have seen a real live person on the landing.

Clenching her pistol, she pulled open the door and stepped outside. The rain came down in giant sheets, reducing visibility to only a couple of feet. Squinting, she leaned forward, trying to see into the brush about twenty feet from the door. Was something moving in there?

A burst of thunder boomed overhead and lightning streaked across the sky, lighting up the entire courtyard. Rays of light streaked through the brush, illuminating the individual branches and leaves. Nothing. But she could have sworn something was there just seconds ago.

The sheets of rain gusted toward her now and the huge

drops stung her face and eyes, causing her vision to blur. Time to go back inside and lock the door behind her.

Then a hand grabbed her shoulder, and she screamed.

Chapter Six

Alaina spun around, gun leveled, and knocked the elderly man down onto the laundry room floor.

"Oh, no!" She tossed her gun onto the sheets and reached down to help the man, who must be the caretaker, to his feet.

"I'm so sorry," she said, scanning him up and down for visible injuries. "Are you all right?"

"Been hit harder." He delivered that single statement, then stood there staring, but in an odd way—not expectantly and not as if he was studying her.

"I'm Alaina LeBeau," she said, breaking the uncomfortable silence. "You must be Amos."

"Yep," he said and continued standing there, water dripping down his face and body and onto the laundry room floor.

All righty, then.

Alaina reached for one of the folded towels she'd washed earlier and handed it to Amos. "I'm sorry about that. I thought I saw someone outside in the courtyard and then when you touched me… I guess I'm feeling a little jumpy."

Amos dried his face with the towel and nodded. "It's a strange house. Has a strange feel. That's why I told Mr.

Purcell I wouldn't live here. Got my own place. It don't feel strange."

Alaina had her doubts that any space Amos occupied would feel normal, but now wasn't the best time to explore that thought. "Did you need something, Amos?"

"Saw lights on. Thought I'd better check things out. Wasn't expecting you till Thursday."

"It *is* Thursday."

"You don't say." He rubbed his chin. "Well, then I guess I lost track of a day or two."

An encouraging thought. "I appreciate your checking on me."

"Just doing my job. Guess now that I have, I'll head off to bed."

"Did you walk over here from your cabin?" Maybe Amos had been the one she saw in the courtyard. That would be the best explanation she could think of.

"In this storm? I'm old, not crazy. I drove my truck over. It's parked out front."

"Do you want to wait here a bit until the storm slacks off?" Good manners forced her to make the offer, but she held her breath, hoping the odd caretaker would take his leave into the monsoon.

"Won't slack anytime soon. Need to get home before the power goes out."

He started down the hallway and across the entry to the front door. Alaina trailed behind him, alternating between relief that he was leaving and worry that she might spend her first night in the swamp mansion of horrors without lights.

"There are flashlights in that cabinet next to the washing machine," Amos said when he stopped at the front door. "I keep working batteries in 'em. You best get a couple soon."

"Thanks. If you get a chance tomorrow, I'd really appreciate it if you can come by and show me around the house and point out anything else I need to know about it."

"Of course. That's my job." He stared at her for a couple of seconds. "You look like your mother."

"That's what people say. I'm afraid my memories of her are hazy."

"No matter. Now that you're here, she'll be by soon and you can see for yourself."

THUNDER BOOMED over the sheriff's department and the lights blinked. Carter logged off the computer before the storm could do it for him. Every time he got shut down by a power outage, it was a pain in the rear to get things working right the next morning.

He'd spent a frustrating two hours after his conversation with William trying to find more-concrete information on Trenton Purcell and Ophelia LeBeau, but there was little to find. That didn't surprise him much in Ophelia's case. She was an heiress and, according to William, had come into millions when her parents passed. But she was a small-town bayou heiress with parents who'd felt no compulsion to be in the limelight of the city or on the front of newspapers hosting some charity event. Based on what he could find, they'd lived a quiet, simple life in a mansion on the bayou and had raised their daughter to live the same way.

Which she'd managed nicely until Trenton Purcell entered her life.

Purcell had been even more of an enigma. Despite extensive searching, Carter had been unable to trace the man back to his birthplace, his parents, previous employment or even a driver's license. All of which made career cops very suspicious.

He'd bet anything he owned that Trenton Purcell was living under an assumed name and identity in Calais, but he had no proof. And at this point, he couldn't see what difference it would make, except to further exasperate people who'd liked Ophelia and warned her off marrying the man.

He locked the sheriff's department and ran to his truck, but he was still soaked by the time he jumped inside. It was really coming down out there. He started down Main Street, but when he got to the intersection at the edge of town, he stopped in the middle of the street. His current residence—a cabin he'd inherited from his grandfather—was to the left, near his mother's house. To the right was the lonely road that led to the LeBeau estate.

He had no obligation to check on Alaina. In fact, she'd probably resent the intrusion more than appreciate it, as their earlier parting hadn't exactly been without conflict. But something tugged at him.

She's a beautiful woman who's all alone.

That much was true, and he could go straight home and try to convince himself that that was all that concerned him. But he'd given up lying years ago—even to himself.

Sighing, he turned the steering wheel to the right. He'd just make a quick stop—only long enough to ensure she was getting on all right in the storm. Then he'd head home for a big bowl of his mother's vegetable soup, heated up in his microwave, and a cold beer.

A visual of Alaina LeBeau climbing the stairwell flashed across his mind. The way her jeans clung to her perfectly toned rear. The way her breasts strained against the cotton blouse as she turned to look back at him.

He blew out a breath.

Maybe two beers were in order. Two beers and a cold shower.

AMOS SLIPPED OUT the front door and into the storm before Alaina found her voice. Not that it mattered. What the hell did you say to follow up a statement like that? If Amos believed her mother was going to show up twenty-five years post-death and speak to her, he was either crazy or suffering from some sort of aging disease.

She locked the door and hurried back to the laundry room to find the flashlights while the lights still worked. Even entombed in the huge house, she could hear the storm intensifying. The rumbles of thunder were closer together than before, and she could hear the plinking sound of heavy drops of rain against the northern glass in the kitchen area. It was time to wrap up her day and lock herself up in the bedroom for the night.

The cabinet door stuck a little and she had to give it a harder tug, then she blew out a breath of relief when the flashlights were right where Amos indicated and in working order. She had a penlight on her key chain, but hadn't even thought to bring anything larger with her. Decades of city living were a definite disadvantage.

She grabbed two of the flashlights and placed them on top of the sheets she'd been folding earlier. Her pistol lay silent and forgotten on the sheets and she quickly put it back in her waistband. The cold metal pressing against her bare skin gave her a bit of comfort and a tiny feeling of security.

She wrapped the ends of the sheets around the flashlights, grabbed the blanket she'd laundered earlier and crept up the spiral staircase, looking around the edge of the big bundle to ensure she didn't misstep on the winding stairs. The absolute last thing she needed was to have an accident. Her cell phone was in her pocket, but she'd bet her last dollar that the storm had knocked out any hope of reception.

Her personal supplies were limited to what she could fit in her SUV, but she'd had enough forethought to pack a mattress cover. It was queen-size and the bed in her old room was full-size, but it would be no problem to tuck the extra under the mattress.

Dust billowed out of the mattress as she lifted the edges to slip the ends of the cover over and dropped them back into place. She waved one hand in the air and covered her face with the other, trying to keep from inhaling the bulk of the flying particles, then alternated tugging one side and then the other until the mattress was completely covered.

She made quick work of the sheets and blanket, then grabbed a flashlight and ran downstairs to snag a bottle of water and a protein bar. It wasn't much of a supper, but it would do for tonight. Back in the bedroom, she shrugged off her jeans and polo shirt and, most important, her bra, in favor of yoga pants and T-shirt. As she lugged her suitcase off the bed, the edge of a folder peeked out at her.

Frowning, she pulled the folder out of her luggage and stared at it for a bit. It had been complete impulse that made her copy the files from the case that had caused her more anguish and guilt than she could bear and had subsequently tanked her career. She'd made a mistake. Somewhere in that file had to be the thing she'd missed. The thing that could have prevented a child's death.

Before she could enter a courtroom again, she had to figure out what that thing was. Had to be certain she wouldn't make the same mistake again. She placed the file on the nightstand next to the bed. The case file might be the only thing that could take her mind off the strangeness of the house, the caretaker and the flashes of memories that she hadn't anticipated and wasn't comfortable with.

Lightning flashed right outside the balcony doors

and she jumped. First thing tomorrow, she had to find something to serve as drapes. Ornate wooden rods were mounted over the French doors, so at one time they had been covered. Likely years of neglect had led to dry rot and the original drapes were long gone.

Thunder rumbled across the sky seconds after the lightning, letting her know the storm was directly above the house. She was beginning to think the pounding would go on forever when she realized the thunder had trailed off and the pounding was coming from downstairs.

She glanced at her watch. Nine o'clock.

She couldn't begin to imagine what someone was doing here so late and in the middle of the storm, but the pounding on the door didn't appear to be slacking off. Amos would have let himself in, so the caretaker was out, and she couldn't imagine the attorney making a trip here this late at night. No one else in Calais had business with her except the sheriff, and he'd already done his duty for the day.

Grabbing her pistol and the flashlight, she hurried downstairs to the front door. "Who is it?" she yelled, hoping her voice projected through the thick wood and over the storm.

"Carter!"

Frowning, she placed the flashlight on the table next to the door and unlocked it.

A burst of wind blew the door open the instant she turned the handle, and she struggled to keep it from banging into the wall. Carter hurried into the house, rain billowing behind him, carried by the wind.

Alaina gave the door a final shove as soon as he cleared it and then stared at the dripping-wet sheriff. "You're making a mess on my floor," she said, pointing at the water pooling around him.

"That's only because the house is so dirty. That rain is going to create mud."

She shook her head. "Are you crazy, coming out here in this storm? Being outside tonight is no place for man or beast."

He ran one hand over his head and then shook his hand to fling off the water. "The storm wasn't so bad when I left. I thought I could beat it."

"Looks like you were wrong. Let me get you a towel before you drown."

She hurried to the laundry room and returned with one of the towels she'd washed earlier.

"Thanks," he said as he rubbed the towel over his head and face and then down his arms.

Alaina couldn't help but notice how the wet T-shirt clung to his arms and chest. It was a display worthy of an underwear advertisement or one of those hunky calendars.

"Is something wrong?" she asked when he finished his wipedown.

"No. Not anything serious. I just thought I'd check on you because of the storm. I wasn't sure you'd have provisions for a power outage. I see you have a flashlight at least."

She nodded. "Amos stopped by earlier and told me where to find them. I guess I wasn't exactly prepared for all this."

"Hard to be when you didn't know what you were walking into. There's a general store in Calais. It's not a large store, but it will have the basic supplies you need."

He passed her the towel and gave her a once-over. "You might want to dry off yourself before you catch a cold."

She glanced down and her breath caught in her throat when she realized that her clothes must have gotten damp from the blowing rain. The thin T-shirt clung to her chest, and without her bra, it left little to the imagination. The hint of a smile on Carter's face made his obvious appreciation clear and she felt a flush run up her neck and onto her face.

Rubbing the towel up and down her arms, she removed the thin layer of rain, then draped the towel around her shoulder and over her breasts. Carter's lips twitched and she was certain her action wasn't lost on the hunky sheriff.

He took a step closer to her and lifted up one end of the towel, his fingers brushing against her breast. "You missed a spot," he said and wiped the end of the towel down the nape of her neck.

She stared at him, frozen, as the soft fibers of the towel brushed across her sensitive skin. Despite logic telling her that getting involved with Carter was the worst idea she'd had in her lifetime, she worried that if he made a move, her body was going to shut her mind off and go along with anything he wanted.

He studied her for a moment, then lowered his mouth to hers, gently brushing her lips with his. Her knees weakened and her mind screamed, *What are you doing?*

She completely ignored the voices in her head and lifted one hand to touch his chest. He wound his fingers through her hair and pulled her closer to him. Then as he began to deepen the kiss, a boom of thunder shook the walls of the house, and instantly, they were pitched into darkness.

Startled by the storm and her completely inappropriate behavior with the sheriff, Alaina dropped her hand and took two steps back to grab the flashlight on the entry table. She clicked it on and shined it toward the hallway ceiling, creating a dim glow in the entry.

It was still enough light to see the amused expression on Carter's face.

She swore under her breath and mentally chided herself for her complete and utter lack of control. Carter knew she was attracted to him—despite her every intention not to be—and probably thought he was well on his way to scoring if the storm hadn't interrupted. The worst part was, she wasn't sure he was wrong.

"If you want me to stay…" he offered.

"No," she said before she could change her mind. "I'm going to lock myself in my room until daylight. Hopefully the power will be back on by morning."

"You're sure?"

"It's just a storm. Believe it or not, we had storms in Baton Rouge, too."

He didn't look convinced, but he was too smart to argue, which only cemented her belief that Carter Trahan read people very well.

"I'll check in sometime tomorrow, depending on what my work schedule allows."

"I'm not going anywhere except into Calais for refrigerated items and, if I get ambitious, some home improvement supplies."

He gave her a single nod and slipped out the front door and into the storm.

Alaina locked the door behind him, then leaned back against it and blew out a breath. So many thoughts were competing for space in her head that it felt as if it would explode. It was time to get a grip.

The utter devastation of the case that had gone all wrong, losing the partnership to an idiot, the memories of this house that she'd never expected to return, the spooky house and strange caretaker… It was all jumbled together in her mind, jockeying for position and leaving her confused and exhausted.

It was no wonder she'd practically thrown herself at

a sexy man. So far, Carter was the only thing about her life that seemed normal. Her intense reaction to him must be because of all the stress and anxiety she was feeling about all the other things.

At least that was what she told herself.

Chapter Seven

Carter took off around the driveway, the truck's tires spinning on the wet stone. He let off the accelerator enough for the tires to grip and then sped away from the house as fast as his field of vision allowed in the downpour.

What the hell had he been thinking?

He'd spent a good ten minutes with William that evening, denying that he had any interest in taking up with a woman. Then at first opportunity, he'd made a move on the worst choice of women in a hundred-mile radius.

Alaina LeBeau was beautiful and her body would make sculptors weep, but she was prickly, inconsistent and abrupt. Even worse, she was off balance and a bit fearful. He had no business taking advantage of her questionable emotional state and no desire to risk the fallout when the fear was gone and she realized exactly what she'd done. He had no doubt that if they'd finished what they'd started, she wouldn't have appreciated it tomorrow morning.

He probably would have appreciated it a little too much.

Which was why beginning right now, he was all business with the heiress. If he felt even a twinge of faltering, he'd just repeat "she's an attorney" over and over again in his mind. If that didn't squelch any amorous feelings, nothing would.

As he made his way down the gravel road that led to his house, he saw lights on in his mother's kitchen. He had no reason to stop—well, other than his mom often made chicken and dumplings on Thursdays—but he turned the steering wheel and pulled his truck under the carport next to his mother's ancient Cadillac.

The gap from the carport to the back door was only a couple of feet, but Carter was still drenched by the time his mother opened the door to let him in.

"Good heavens," she said, and hurried to the laundry room, then returned with a clean towel. "What in the world are you doing out in this storm? I swear, sometimes I think I didn't do such a good job raising you."

Carter took the towel and dried off, trying not to think about the last time he'd been in a situation with a towel and a wet body. The whole point of stopping at his mother's house was to put his thoughts back into perspective.

The smell of chicken broth wafted by, making his mouth water. "Your chicken and dumplings are worth getting a little wet." He grinned and handed her the towel.

She shook her head, but he could tell she was pleased with the compliment. "Sit down, then," she said as she carried the towel back to the laundry room. "I'll fix you a bowl."

She scooped him a huge serving of dumplings into a bowl and placed it in front of him along with a beer. "You look like you could use a drink, but William had the last of my whiskey."

He smiled. "No one knows me like you do, Mom."

She slid into the chair next to him. "That's true, which is why I know that you didn't come here for supper, even though I'd be the first to agree that my chicken and dumplings are first-rate. So are you going to tell me what's wrong or do I have to ground you until you talk?"

He stuck a huge dumpling in his mouth and held up one finger. Absolutely amazing.

His mother shook her head. "You know, if you'd find yourself a woman who cooks, you might get a decent meal other than the nights you stop here."

He popped the top on the beer and took a swig. "I have three women, to be exact—all working down at the café. They provide me with home-cooked meals and I provide them with a good portion of my paycheck."

"You get a wife and she could provide you with a lot more than food."

"I'm not having this conversation with you."

"What conversation?"

"The one about all the things a wife could provide me with. Some of those aren't the sort of thing you think about sitting at the dinner table with your mother."

She waved a hand in dismissal. "You think I don't know anything? Your father and I had forty glorious years together and we darn sure didn't spend them all watching television. Do you still think the stork dropped you off?"

He stared at his mother in dismay. "Can we just change the subject? Please?"

"Fine. So if it's not woman troubles, then what's got you out this late in the middle of a downpour?"

He tried to formulate a response that didn't include Alaina LeBeau but couldn't come up with anything.

"Aha!" His mom clapped her hands. "I knew it was a woman."

He dropped his fork in the bowl and sighed. It was absolutely useless to try to hide things from his mom. Her uncanny ability to read people had left him little wiggle room as a child and it sometimes seemed even less as an adult.

"Alaina LeBeau arrived today."

His mother studied him for a couple of seconds. "I see. How does she look?"

"She looks like a city lawyer."

She smiled. "Beautiful, then. William said she favored her mother, so I expected as much."

"Her looks are not the problem."

"So there *is* a problem."

"The beautiful, cast-off daughter of an heiress turns up decades later after her evil stepfather's death to live in the big mansion of horrors, and you have to ask if there's a problem."

"So she *is* beautiful."

He sighed. "Can we stick to the problem part, please?"

"Of course. I was just trying to get my facts straight."

"Uh-huh." He took another bite of the dumplings and began to tell his mother about his first meeting with Alaina, his concern that someone else had been in the house, his subsequent conversation with William and the lack of readily available information on Trenton Purcell. He left out the part about his second visit. It wasn't relevant to the case.

His mother frowned when he was done and tapped one finger on the breakfast table. "I don't like it," she finally said.

"Me either, but I'm at a loss as to what to do about it. I have nothing concrete to go on—no direction in which to focus."

"So I take you didn't get anything further in your second visit with Alaina?"

He stared. "How did you— Never mind. No, I didn't

find out anything except that the power was off and Amos told her where to find flashlights."

"You should have stuck around, at least until the storm passed."

"I offered, but she turned me down."

His mother raised one eyebrow.

"Scout's honor," he said.

"You were always a horrible scout. Gave the scout leaders fits, but you are my son, so I suppose you made the offer. Makes me wonder about the girl, though."

"Why is that?"

"If a fine-looking man offered to keep me company in an unfamiliar and creepy house during the rainstorm of the century, I would have taken him up on it."

He smiled. "You're great for a man's ego."

She patted his hand with hers. "I'm just telling it like it is."

ALAINA LOCKED the bedroom door and checked it twice before moving to the patio doors to check them again. The doors were secure, both flashlights were working and her pistol was handily positioned on one of the nightstands next to the bed. She'd forgone the protein bar in favor of a peanut butter sandwich, chips and too many chocolate chip cookies, but she would worry about the calories tomorrow. Or not.

Likely, the stress of spending the night in this house would burn off half of what she ate, and the stress of figuring out how to stop turning into a wanton woman around Carter Trahan would burn off the other half.

She stacked pillows against the headboard and snagged her plate of food from the top of the dresser where she'd placed it earlier. The sheets were crisp and cool against her bare arms. Normally, she'd be relishing the refreshing, clean fabric against her legs, but given the uncertain nature of everything, she thought it would be prudent to keep her yoga pants on. If there was an emergency, the last thing she needed was to leap over the balcony and run down the road in her T-shirt and underwear, despite having seen a woman do exactly that at least twice on late-night movies the week before.

She nestled back against the pillows and took a bite of her sandwich, wishing she had a television—that and the power to run it—and cable. Watching television wasn't often on her list of things to do, but she usually had the set running in her condo back in Baton Rouge just to break the silence, especially when she had trouble sleeping. Right now, she'd give up cookies for a month if she could switch on some mindless late-night show and lose herself in the babble.

Chiding herself for not thinking to bring a book, she reached for the file she'd left on the nightstand, but it was on the far edge just out of her reach. Staring at the folder, she frowned. Hadn't she left it on the edge of the nightstand closest to the bed? She could have sworn that was the case.

She stiffened and her pulse picked up a beat in her temples as she scanned the room to see if anything else was out of place. Suitcase, laptop, clothes from earlier, shoes…all appeared to be right where she'd left them.

You're spooking yourself.

Yes, that was it. That had to be it. Still, she fought the urge to climb out of bed and check the locks she knew she'd checked right before getting into bed. She had fourteen days to manage here. Paranoia would make it feel like a hundred.

She leaned over to grab the folder, then relaxed against the pillows again, forcing her mind to switch gears.

You can do this. No one is as hardheaded as you.

She placed the folder on the bed beside her, opened it and lifted the first paper out of the stack to begin reading while she finished her supper. Soon, she was so caught up in reviewing the case file that she didn't even realize she'd finished her sandwich, chips and every single one of the cookies until her fingers brushed against only an empty plate.

Everything in her notes so far was exactly as she'd remembered—exactly as she'd read a thousand times and committed to memory. Nothing gave even the most remote indication that the teen she was defending was a sociopathic serial rapist and murderer. She'd replayed every single meeting with him in her mind a million times and watched the video of the sessions over and over again, looking for something she missed.

She'd never found anything.

But she must have missed something, because the alternative wasn't acceptable. If someone so young could fool her so absolutely and completely, she wasn't fit to do her job. Logically, she knew he'd fooled everyone, including his teachers, employer, doctors, his parents and most important, the jury, but that fact did nothing to alleviate her guilt.

She slid the empty plate onto the nightstand and reached for the next set of documents. This was it, she promised herself. She'd read every document in the file one more time, then she'd force herself to let it go. Sometimes, bad things happened. Maybe this was one of those times.

She lifted the next document and began to read, unaware of when she dropped off to sleep. Her only memory was the steady hum of rain on the roof and her eyes growing fuzzy.

THE BEDROOM wasn't the same when she opened her eyes. A lantern on the dresser cast a dim glow over the room. She could still hear the rain falling on the roof, but the bed was narrower and the sheets silk rather than cotton. A rustling sound caught her attention and she looked toward the bedroom wall where the sound had originated.

Her baby sister tossed and turned in her sleep. Her fine locks of hair were damp from the humidity the storm had driven in, and clung to her pale skin. She turned to the left and saw her middle sister, curled in a ball in the twin bed next to her, her pink blanket kicked to the floor long ago.

It must have been a dream that had woken her, she thought as she turned over and closed her eyes again. Then she heard the voices. Mommy and the mean man were arguing again. It happened often, after she and her sisters had gone to bed. They probably thought she couldn't hear in that big house, but sometimes their voices carried all the way to the sisters' bedroom.

She pulled the covers over her head, trying to block out the arguing. Mommy was unhappy with the mean man—she was certain—but every time Alaina thought Mommy would make him leave, she was disappointed. Daddy had never made Mommy cry or raise her voice. Daddy had loved her and her sisters and was never cross or stern with them.

Daddy was in heaven and couldn't come back. Mommy had told them that, so it must be true. But Alaina would have been happier with just Mommy. Not as happy as she'd been before Daddy went to heaven, but almost as happy.

Out of the corner of her eye, she saw something move and she threw back the covers, figuring her sister had heard the arguing, too.

But she wasn't prepared at all for what she saw.

ALAINA BOLTED UPRIGHT in bed, her eyes locked on to the ethereal figure from her dreams that hovered above her bed near the ceiling. Lightning struck the tree outside the bedroom window, sounding off like a sonic boom.

But her scream was even louder.

Chapter Eight

It wasn't even daylight when Alaina pressed her foot down on her SUV's accelerator and launched it as fast as safely possible down the road to Calais. She'd seen a café on Main Street as she'd driven through town the day before. Surely it would be open soon. If not, she'd sit in her SUV until it did. Now or an hour from now, coffee was the first order of business. Coffee and a heavy dose of sanity.

After her ghostly sighting, she'd run out of the house and spent the rest of the night sleeping in her SUV. Her neck and back ached from being in the same position so long and she was more exhausted than she'd ever been before—including law school or when working an important case.

Just minutes ago, she'd managed to go back into the still-dark house long enough to change clothes, but the thought of thirteen more days and nights locked up in that house with whatever that was in there with her had her rethinking her inheritance. She didn't need the money, whatever it turned out to be. Per the stipulations in the will, she wouldn't even find out the worth of the estate until she fulfilled her end of the bargain. And even then, her sisters had to be located and agree to the same ridiculous concession in order for any of them to collect.

You made a mistake.

The thought always lingered in the back of her mind, picking its way through like a splinter. She'd managed to keep it at bay for a week—convincing herself that quitting her job and moving off to the middle of the bayou was a great plan—but she could no longer ignore the thought. Maybe she'd been too hasty with her career. She could have sucked it up and stayed where she was while putting out feelers for positions with other firms. Sure, Peterson, Winstrom and Wilson was the most prestigious in Baton Rouge, but it wasn't as if she had ties to that city. New Orleans had always been fun to visit. She could have moved there, or out of state…maybe back to New England, where her law school friends had settled into successful careers.

She blew out a breath. All of that was hindsight, which didn't do her any good. She had to face the situation in front of her and decide if she wanted to chuck it all now. At least she would only have lost a couple of days. Not to mention leaving now would likely improve her health. Living in Calais was certain to cause her high blood pressure, maybe even a heart attack.

A bit of relief coursed through her when she saw the lit Open sign in the café window. A small building with lights and people was exactly what she needed to get her back to normal. When she wasn't panicked, she could make decisions.

A pretty, young waitress greeted her when she walked into the otherwise-empty café. "Take a seat anywhere. The cook's late as usual, but I've got a fresh pot of coffee almost ready. You interested?"

"Absolutely," she said and slipped onto a stool at a bar in front of the grill, wanting to be near the only other person in the room.

The waitress smiled and poured her a cup of the steaming liquid. "You must be Alaina," she said as she set the coffee in front of her. "My name's Connie."

Alaina stared at her for a moment.

"Small town," Connie explained. "Your arrival is big news and even if everyone in here yesterday wasn't talking about it, I would know you weren't from here anyway. I know everyone in Calais. Took me all of four days to meet the whole town when I first moved here."

Alaina smiled. "Four whole days?"

"The Johnsons were on vacation or it would have been faster."

Alaina laughed, feeling more at ease in the company of this pleasant woman. "I guess I haven't settled into the small-town role yet."

"I have to admit it took a bit of getting used to. I've lived mostly in cities, where you can get robbed on the street in broad daylight and everyone will pretend they didn't see. In Calais, a new haircut is worth at least thirty minutes of breakfast conversation."

"Then I guess I'll disappoint everyone. I had a haircut right before I left."

Connie poured herself a cup of coffee and took a big sip, then leaned on the counter in front of Alaina. "How was your first night in the house?"

Alaina felt her stomach clench. "It was fine," she said, hoping her voice sounded normal.

Connie stared at her for a moment. "You sure?"

"Why do you ask?"

"Because when you came in here, you looked like you'd seen a ghost."

Alaina set her coffee cup down too hard and coffee sloshed over the edge of the cup and splashed onto her hand.

"Oh!" Connie turned around and scooped a piece of

ice out of the cooler behind her. She wrapped it in a thin dishrag and handed it to Alaina. "I am so sorry. I didn't mean to startle you."

Alaina placed the cool rag against the red spot on the back of her hand and instantly felt some of the pain dissipate. "It's not your fault," she assured the clearly distraught waitress. "I might have exaggerated my comfort level with the house just a bit."

"We have some ointment in the back and some bandages."

Alaina lifted the cloth to inspect her hand. "It's fine." She held up her hand toward Connie to show her that the tiny pink spot was all that was left.

"Thank goodness," Connie said as she studied Alaina's hand. "Burns are nasty and will bother you at the most inconvenient times."

"I've been fortunate to only have the occasional hair-implement burn, but then I'm not much of a cook. I bet working with food, you've seen more than your share."

Connie nodded. "A basic hazard of the job. I've gotten good at avoiding most problems, but then, I've been at this since I was a teen."

She stopped speaking for a couple of seconds and Alaina could see the indecision in her expression. Finally, she spoke again. "Do you want to talk about it? I mean, whatever spooked you? I know I'm basically a stranger, but I was new in town not long ago. I know how your mind can work against you in a new place."

Alaina gave her a rueful smile. "I can't imagine you nervous anywhere. You seem so collected."

"I have my moments. Had one my first night in Calais. I rent a cabin from your mother's estate. I think a groundskeeper lived there years ago. If you take a left at that last split in the road on the way to the big house, the cabin I'm renting is another two miles down a dirt road into the middle of the swamp."

"Oh, I didn't realize there were other structures beyond the main house and the caretaker's cabin, but then, I was very young when I left. I suppose the living situation of staff wouldn't have been on a seven-year-old's mind."

"I'm sure it wouldn't."

"So I take it your cabin is as remote as the main house. Is it as run-down?"

"The first time I drove out there, I was convinced it was at least a mile past the end of the earth, but everything was in working order. It took me several days to get it cleaned to my liking, but at least no critters had moved in while it was vacant."

Connie hesitated a moment, then said, "I guess you weren't as lucky."

"So far, everything seems to be working, but I didn't have time to test it all before the storm blew in and knocked out the power. It definitely hasn't seen the backside of a dusting cloth in ages. And so far, I haven't seen any critters."

"But?"

Alaina sighed. In the bright lights of the café, she felt a little silly about her fear. "I overthought everything and spooked myself."

"That's what you think now, but when you walked in here, you were debating driving straight out of town after breakfast."

"How…how did you know that?"

Connie shrugged. "I've gotten good at reading people." She gave her a sheepish smile. "Besides, I have some experience in that area. Let's just say I'm not exactly used to the night sounds of the swamp. I spent my first two nights sleeping in my car behind the café."

Alaina felt some of the tension leave her back. "I spent last night in my SUV in the driveway. If it hadn't been storming so hard, I might have driven away then."

"It took some getting used to for me, and I have only eight hundred square feet to be comfortable in. It's no wonder you got spooked in that big old house. I think I saw the place on a late-night horror movie."

Alaina laughed. "That's exactly as I'd describe it. It really works the imagination. When you combine that with the drive, the storm and the fact that I'm still trying to absorb the oddity of the entire situation, I guess it did a number on me."

Connie nodded. "I can imagine." She pulled a pad of paper from her apron and jotted a phone number on it.

"Here's my cell number," she said and handed Alaina the piece of paper. "It's probably useless in a storm, but if you need anything, I'm probably closest."

"Thank you." Alaina took the paper and stuck it in her wallet, a bit overwhelmed by the compassion of this woman who was essentially a stranger. "That's very nice of you."

"I know what it's like to be the new girl in town."

Alaina smiled. "If you don't mind my asking, how in the world did you end up here?"

"I'd been working at a restaurant on Bourbon Street and it was my day off. I wanted to get out of the city— away from all the crowds of people—so I just started driving. I ended up here around lunchtime and liked the feel of the place and the food. Then one of the longtime waitresses quit right in front of me to follow a long-haul trucker to Mississippi and I thought, *Why the heck not?* I guess it sounds a little crazy."

"Not to me. And if it worked out for you, then it was good to go with your gut."

Connie nodded. "At first, I was nervous, having never lived in a place this small before, but the people here are great and they look out for each other. It's not what I'm used to, but it's nice." She peered over Alaina's shoulder and out the café storefront. "Here comes one of Calais's finest."

Alaina glanced back just as Carter exited his truck. She whipped back around and Connie raised her eyebrows.

"I take it you've met the sexy sheriff?" she asked.

"He's my babysitter," Alaina said. "His words, not mine."

"Hmm. I'd find statements like that a bit irritating, but it wouldn't diminish his hotness any."

"Go for it."

"No way. He's not my type."

"Sexy isn't your type?"

Connie laughed. "Serious and narrowly focused isn't my type. Law enforcement guys tend to be married to their jobs."

The bell over the café door jangled and Alaina heard footsteps behind her, then Carter slid onto the stool next to her.

"You're in my spot," he said with a smile, "but I'll allow it this time as you're new in town."

Connie rolled her eyes at Alaina, then turned to pour him a cup of coffee.

"You're up early," he said as Connie slid the coffee in front of him. "Was everything okay last night? Has the power come back on yet?"

You imagined it.

She was going to keep thinking it until she believed it. The last thing she needed was Carter reporting back to the estate attorney that the heiress was crazy.

"Things were okay. The storm was a bit intense and

the power's still off, but I'm hoping it's on by the time I head back."

He nodded. "A couple of power lines are down, but a crew was already working on them when I drove past. It shouldn't take long."

She shrugged, trying to appear casual about the whole thing even though she didn't feel that way. "I have nothing to hurry over. I'll sit here and have a good breakfast—assuming the cook ever shows up—and then make a trip to the store to get some supplies."

"Sounds like a good plan. Except for the cook part." He looked over at Connie, who was refilling salt shakers. "Jack isn't here yet?"

Purcell's former errand boy had fallen in love with a local widow six months before and decided to make a go of the straight life. He'd been fortunate to get a chance cooking at the café.

"No. Ten minutes after is normal, but it's thirty past now." She frowned. "The past week, though, it seems he's been pushing later every day."

Carter sighed. "He's drinking again."

Connie's eyes widened. "I didn't say that."

"You didn't have to. I've known Jack my whole life. I'll drop by this evening and have a talk with him."

"If he's got a real problem," Alaina said, "it probably won't do any good."

"No," Carter agreed, "but when my mom asks if I've spoken to Jack, I can say yes with a clear conscience and not have to endure her disapproval."

Alaina smiled. "I think I like your mother."

"Everyone likes Mrs. Trahan," Connie said. "She's absolutely fabulous."

The back door of the café slammed and a couple of seconds later, a scruffy man—probably in his mid-forties—

walked up to the grill and turned it on. Then he reached for the coffeepot and poured himself a huge cup. Alaina saw his hands shaking a bit as he poured.

"And good morning to you, sunshine," Connie said.

Jack barely turned and mumbled a hello before starting to oil the grill. But it was long enough for Alaina to catch a glimpse of his bloodshot eyes. She glanced over at Carter and saw him frowning. He'd been right about the drinking.

Connie forced a smile. "Can I get you guys some breakfast?"

"I'll have the special," Carter said.

Alaina glanced at the menu and nodded. "I'll have the special, as well." Two eggs, toast, bacon and hash browns sounded like a great way to start the morning, especially because her dinner had consisted of peanut butter, chips and cookies.

Connie took the orders and handed them to the cook before heading away from the bar to take care of a group of men who'd just walked in. Alaina looked down at her coffee to avoid Carter's gaze, wishing she could move somewhere else to eat without looking incredibly rude. It hadn't been so bad when Connie was there in the midst of the conversation, but Alaina didn't really want to talk to the sexy sheriff one-on-one.

"So," Carter said, "William tells me you resigned from your position with the firm in Baton Rouge to come here. Wouldn't they let you take a leave of absence?"

Great. Aside from what she thought she saw last night and her unwanted attraction to Carter, he'd managed to ask about the only other thing she had no desire to talk about—her job.

"I suppose they may have given me a leave," she said,

not about to tell him she'd quit before finding out about the inheritance, "but I didn't ask."

"So you just walked away from the most prestigious firm in Baton Rouge—per William—to meet the completely irregular requirements of a will, even though if your sisters don't also meet the requirements, it will turn out to be a complete waste of your time."

"Yes."

"Okay, then. Don't bother with the details. I'll just go on wondering if you're mental."

Alaina felt her frustration rise. She imagined quite a few people thought the same thing Carter did. And even though it seemed that way on the surface, it rankled her that people immediately jumped to her being flighty and irrational with her decision to resign her position. Especially when men did it. Men couldn't possibly understand what women were up against with the good ol' boy network. They were biologically prevented from getting it on anything but a surface level.

"I wasn't aware that sharing my personal business was part of the stipulations of the inheritance. But if that's the case, then I have to assume that goes for you as well because you're part of this bizarre requirement. Mr. Duhon tells me that you're quite good at your job because of all the experience you gained from being a detective with the New Orleans Police Department. So why would you leave a solid career path like that to come back to Calais and babysit heiresses?"

Carter's jaw flexed and Alaina could tell he wasn't happy with the turnaround, but as he opened his mouth to speak, Connie cleared her throat and slid their breakfast in front of them.

"Ketchup or Tabasco?" Connie asked.

"No, thank you," Alaina said as Carter shook his head.

"If you don't mind," he said, "I'm going to eat my breakfast with the fishermen. I need to talk to them about some vandalism at the shrimp house."

He slid his plate off the counter and headed across the café before she could even formulate a response. Which was probably just as well because she was having trouble coming up with anything that didn't imply he was a coward for avoiding her question. It seemed the good sheriff liked information only when he was receiving it, not giving it.

"I'm sorry for the interruption," Connie said, "but things looked a little intense."

Alaina watched as Carter greeted the men at a table near the front of the café, then turned back to face Connie. "I should be the one apologizing. The last thing you need to deal with at work is two adults who can't keep their tempers in check."

Connie glanced over at Carter, then looked back at Alaina. "I don't think I've ever seen him that flustered before. His blood pressure is usually so low that I sometime want to hold a mirror in front of his mouth to see if he's still breathing."

"It seems to be a talent of mine," Alaina said, recalling her conversation with Everett that precipitated her resignation. "I have the unique ability to find the exact words to tick men off."

"Hmm, you know, if it makes them mad, it's only because you've struck a nerve."

"Perhaps, but Sheriff Trahan's nerves are none of my concern, much less striking them."

Connie gave her a mischievous grin. "I don't know. You could do a lot worse than setting off some nerve endings in that man. He looks very…capable."

"No, thank you."

"What? You don't like capable men?"

"Capable but inflexible men have been my downfall recently—professionally and personally. I'm on hiatus until I do a better job with discernment."

Connie sighed and nodded. "I completely understand."

She told herself not to do it, but Alaina couldn't seem to stop herself from glancing back once more. At that exact moment, Carter turned his head and their eyes locked. She held his gaze, refusing to be the first to look away, then he winked. She jerked her head back around and stabbed her eggs with her fork.

Darn it. She'd been the first to flinch.

Chapter Nine

Alaina watched as a nice teen boy loaded the third and last box of supplies into her SUV. She tried to hand him some money after he closed the car door, but he shook his head.

"We can't take tips, Ms. LeBeau, but I appreciate the thought. Is there anything else I can help you with?"

"Not today, Sam. But I reserve the right to have you load more of those cheesecakes if I really like the one I bought today."

The dark-haired teen gave her a shy smile. "It would be my pleasure. You have a nice day now."

"You, too." She jumped into her SUV and backed out of the parking space in front of the general store. When she reached the end of town and turned onto the first of the three roads that would carry her away from civilization and back into the depths of the swamp, her cell phone rang.

She pulled it out of the side pocket of her purse and frowned at the display when she saw the number for the law firm. It was highly unlikely they were calling to beg her to return to her position and impossible that they would offer her the partnership, so she started to toss the phone onto the passenger's seat without answering. More likely, they wanted her to answer a question about one of the cases she'd been assisting on so they could avoid doing any actual research themselves.

Finally, curiosity won out and she answered the call.

"Alaina." Everett's voice sounded agitated and somewhat surprised. "I wasn't sure I'd be able to reach you given the remote location."

"Service seems to come and go, so you may want to get anything important out as soon as possible." And if she didn't deem it important, she'd just end the call and pretend it was bad service.

"There's been a situation here, and the police felt I should alert you."

"The police… What kind of situation?" All of her current cases had been boring business lawsuits. Nothing dangerous about them.

"There was some vandalism."

"At the firm?"

"No, to my car."

Alaina held in a sigh. "So why do the police think I need to know about that?"

"Because of the note left on the windshield. It said 'All of you will pay.' There were no fingerprints."

Alaina clenched the steering wheel as she drew up to the stop sign. "You think it has something to do with the Warren case?"

"It's possible. The police think that for someone to make that kind of threat, the situation had to be serious. I can't think of anything else the firm has handled lately that would have warranted that sort of attack."

Mentally, she ran through the cases the firm had handled the past twelve months, trying to come up with another alternative, but she couldn't think of a single option where emotions had run beyond irritated. Certainly no one had left court angry enough to issue threats.

"The police are investigating?" she asked.

"Yes, but short of checking alibis for the most logical perpetrators, there's not much else they can do with the limited amount of evidence available."

"Then what do they recommend I do?"

"They seem to think remaining in your current situation is the most logical choice. Very few people know where you are, and we've already alerted everyone at the firm as to the importance of keeping your whereabouts a secret."

"Okay. As soon as you get more information—"

"I'll contact you as soon as I know more."

"The cell service is questionable at best when I'm at the house, and nonexistent in storms, which I've been informed are quite common here. If you can't reach me, will you please contact the sheriff, Carter Trahan?"

"Making friends with law enforcement already?"

"As part of the rules of the estate, Carter will check in with me daily. And if trouble is coming my way, he'd need to know anyway."

"Fine, then. I'll be in touch as soon as I know more."

A horn sounded behind Alaina and she jumped. Then she realized she'd been sitting still at the stop sign during the entire call. She tossed her cell phone on the passenger's seat and waved an apology before turning right to head toward the house.

The road narrowed almost immediately and the trees seemed to crowd the thin path into the swamp. She took a deep breath and blew it out, trying to process this latest turn of events. The last thing she needed was something else to worry about—something else that would have her looking over her shoulder all the time.

Why now?

The trial was over a year ago and the...other...happened

right after. If the people who blamed her for the situation were going to come after her and Everett, wouldn't they have done it right after the murder?

She forced the last word into her mind. It was time to call it like it was and stop shading it with gray. That case was one of the things she'd promised herself she would deal with during this break. Facing it head-on was long overdue and was a requirement if she planned to have any future at all in criminal law.

Murder.

Saying the word—even silently—made her stomach roll.

If one silently repeated word made her feel so sick, how must the parents feel? How much did they hate her? How much did they blame her for what happened? The girl's mother had turned up at the law office a week after, accosting Alaina as she walked from the high-rise parking and into the building. She'd called her names and spit on her.

Alaina had reported the incident to Everett and the police, but she'd refused to file charges. It was hard to blame the woman for her anger, especially when part of her agreed with the things the woman had said.

As she pulled through the overgrown driveway of the house, she took it in again with a critical eye. It was a wreck, which certainly didn't help to create feelings of comfort and ease, and the remote location, spectacular storms and questionable security all piled on to create mild paranoia. It would be easy to go over the edge of paranoia and into panic.

That was what had happened to her last night, but she was determined that it wouldn't happen again.

She parked directly in front of the front doors and unlocked them before lugging the refrigerated groceries, stepladder and wallpaper-removal supplies inside. First up was a cleaning spree. It would take months to get it all clean and far longer to make all the necessary repairs, but if her sisters were located and agreed to the terms of the will, then this property would become theirs. The work needed to be done and she needed the distraction. Not to mention, the house might not appear so spooky if it wasn't so dismal.

The cold items went directly to the refrigerator—one of the rare clean places in the house—but she left the rest of the supplies in the entry along with the cleaning supplies she'd unloaded the night before. The kitchen was first on her cleaning list and the fewer things in the way, the easier the task would be.

Once the refrigerated items were stored away, she lugged the heavy box of cleaning supplies into the kitchen and then hurried upstairs to change. The bedroom was a mess from her dramatic night and departure. Papers from the case file had slid off the bed and scattered across the floor. Her yoga pants and sleeping shirt hung from the bedpost, and the paper plate and cup from her dinner were still perched on the nightstand.

She took the time to pick up the papers from the floor and lay them on the unmade bed, but anything else would wait. The kitchen was her first priority. She wanted at least one place in the house where she could sit and not feel as dreary as the room. The bedroom wasn't a good choice. If another room had been as secure, she would never have chosen her childhood room. Likely, memories trickling in were a big part of the reason she felt so much uneasiness.

She shrugged off her jeans and polo shirt and pulled on the old sweats and T-shirt she kept for dirty projects. The humidity already had her hair clinging to the back of her neck, so she unzipped a pocket on her purse and dug for one of the hair bands she usually kept in the pocket with her flash drive. Feeling around, her fingers brushed against the bands, but the case for the flash drive wasn't there.

She placed her purse on the bed and opened it up wide to peer inside. She scooped everything out of the pocket but the flash drive was nowhere in sight. Panicked, she turned the purse upside down and dumped all the contents onto the bed. Her entire life was stored on that flash drive—account numbers, passwords, contacts—it was her portable backup and she never went anywhere without it.

She pushed the pile of objects around on the blanket to spread it out, scanning for the flash drive. When she brushed her wallet out of the way, a pink rubber case gleamed, and she let out a breath she'd been holding. She pulled the tab off the case and peered inside. The flash drive was tucked inside as always.

Shaking her head, she scooped up everything and dumped it back into her purse but continued to hold the flash drive, trying to remember everything from the day before. Prior to leaving Baton Rouge, she'd backed up her laptop onto the flash drive, then put it back in her purse. She was certain she'd zipped it into the pocket as usual. It was as ingrained in her movement as breathing.

Had she removed the drive after arriving at the house?

No, that couldn't be the case. Her laptop was still zipped in its case, closed in her shoulder bag and sitting on top of the dresser. She'd had no reason to remove the flash drive and certainly not to relocate it in her purse.

The anxiety she'd worked so hard at putting to rest hit her again with full force. Had the person who'd vandalized Everett's car found her? Instead of a blatant display, were they choosing instead to keep her on edge until— what? The "what?" part bothered her a lot.

Still clutching the flash drive, she flopped onto the bed. She should pack her bags, leave this house and forget she'd ever heard of William Duhon and Calais, Louisiana. All of this was way more than she'd bargained for. When she'd agreed to come to Calais, her worst fear was of being bored. Now her fears were much more vivid and a much bigger threat to her physically.

She stared out the bedroom door and down the hallway, and the dust began to fade away.

A gold runner with embroidered roses ran down the hallway, the perfect complement to the oak-paneled walls. A decorator table with beautiful ornate legs held a crystal vase that was shaped like a tulip on top. The rustle of a skirt tickled her ears and she saw her mother step into the hallway from the landing, her long, pale pink skirt swishing around her slender legs as she walked.

Her mother looked into their bedroom and smiled at them, her pleasure in her children clearly shown in her expression.

And then the vision was gone.

A single tear slid out of Alaina's eye and down her face. How could she have forgotten how beautiful her mother was? Granted, she didn't have even so much as a locket photo of her, but why couldn't she remember her so vividly before now?

She swiped the tear from her cheek and sighed. Everyone who'd known her mother said Alaina looked like her, but they were just being nice. Her mother had the kind of looks men fought wars over. Certainly men responded to Alaina's looks, but none had even had so much as a scuffle, much less a war.

You've forgotten me.

Her mother seemed to speak to her, and she felt a rush of guilt pass over her and began to cry.

"No," she said, looking down the dirty hallway, "I haven't forgotten. I pushed you back—far back in my mind so that the hurt would go away—but I never forgot you. I never stopped loving you."

Wiping the tears from her face with her hand, she rose from the bed, certain of what she had to do. Her mother had loved this home and cherished her family. No way was someone going to scare Alaina away from the only thing she had left of the childhood she'd loved.

She zipped the flash drive back in its purse pocket and headed downstairs. A lot of work lay before her if she wanted to restore this house to how it used to be. And even though the logical part of her didn't believe in spirits and haunts, she could feel her mother's smile upon her.

CARTER TIMED HIS ROUNDS so that he was back on Main Street when Jack got off from work at the café. The widow he'd taken up with had two little girls and the last thing Carter wanted to do was confront Jack in front of any of them. Certainly, the widow knew he was drinking, but there was no point in dragging innocent children into adult business. Not if it could be helped.

He parked at the end of Main Street, then walked around behind the buildings to catch Jack in the alley. His timing was perfect because just as he walked up to the back of the café, the door swung open and Jack walked out.

The cook drew up short when he saw Carter standing there, then frowned. "Something wrong back here?" he asked.

"I was hoping you could tell me that," Carter said.

"Everything's right as rain with me," Jack said, but

the scowl on his face and the fact that he wouldn't meet Carter's eyes said otherwise.

"Then why are you drinking again?"

Jack raised his head and glared at Carter. "Ain't no business of yours what a man does in his free time."

"It is if that man's driving drunk. If I'd have tested you this morning when you arrived at the café, I bet I would have had to haul you in."

"I wasn't drunk and you can't prove it."

Carter sighed. "What the hell are you doing, Jack? I thought you wanted to turn your life around for that woman and her girls. Drunk is no example to set for kids. You, of all people, ought to know that."

"My dad ain't got nothing to do with this either."

"Doesn't he? Remember how your dad looked to you? Do you really want to look that way to those girls?"

A flush crept up Jack's neck. "Who are you to talk with your perfect parents and perfect life? I've had to scrape for everything my whole life. All my problems shoulda been solved when that bastard Purcell died, but he lied, and you're helping that woman get what should have been mine."

Carter sighed. "Purcell promised that you'd inherit, didn't he?"

"Damn right he did. Told me that my family would be set for life. Paid me peanuts all those years, running up and down these roads like a courier, then he died and I got nothing. That broad gets everything and she never once took care of the old man."

"That woman was cast away from here by Purcell when her mother died—separated from her sisters and sent to live with strangers. At seven years old, she hardly had a choice, and I'm of the opinion that those girls got screwed worse than you. Bottom line is that Purcell lied to you.

He knew that the estate would go to Ophelia's children when he died."

"You think I don't know that now? But what good does it do me? Ophelia's daughters will get everything and my daughter will still be sick in her bed because I can't afford the specialist in New Orleans she needs to see."

Carter frowned. He'd heard that one of the children had respiratory problems, but he hadn't known how serious it was. Apparently, Jack had been counting on money from Purcell's estate to pay for the treatment. No wonder he was livid.

"I'm sorry, Jack. What Purcell did to you was wrong, but Ophelia's children aren't to blame for that. Only Purcell is."

"Whatever."

"And drinking isn't going to solve any of your problems. That girl and her mother need you to be strong, now more than ever."

Jack glared. "I'm plenty strong. You'll see."

The cook whirled around and strode off to his car. He gunned the engine as he pulled away, the tires scattering dirt and gravel behind them. Carter watched him drive off, not the least bit happy with the situation. He hoped Jack wouldn't be stupid enough to harass Alaina, but with his drinking again, there was no way to be sure.

When Jack's headlights disappeared around the corner of the alley, Carter headed back to his truck. As soon as he got a chance, he needed to check on Alaina and make her aware of the situation with Jack. If she planned on frequenting the café, she needed to know that the cook wasn't likely to treat her well.

ALAINA BARELY HEARD her cell phone over the iPod she had blasting in her ear. She dropped the mop and dashed for the kitchen counter where she'd left her phone, pulling out her earbuds as she ran. She grabbed the phone and answered without even looking at the display, but all she heard was static.

She glanced down at the display and frowned. The call was from the law firm. All of her cases had been passed off to other attorneys or were being handled by Everett, so there was no reason for anyone to call about business. Which meant it was personal. She pressed Redial, but the same static cut off the call after the first ring.

Glancing outside, she saw thick clouds hanging over the swamp. It wasn't raining here, but she'd bet it was somewhere close by. She tossed the cell phone back on the counter and blew out a breath. If Everett was calling again so soon, he must have more information about the vandal. Maybe they'd caught him.

Or he'd struck again.

Either way, that still put the perp in Baton Rouge, not Calais. Whatever Everett had to tell her could wait until she got a better signal. If it was important, he would call Carter, who'd have no problem driving out to the estate and raining on her parade.

Mind made up, she stepped over to the refrigerator and pulled out a bottled water. The air-conditioning in the house worked surprisingly well, but with the rain clouds hovering, the humidity was sky-high. Seventy-five degrees felt like eighty-five. She ran the cold bottle across her forehead, relishing the cool plastic against her hot skin.

"You've been busy." Amos's voice sounded behind her.

She turned around as the caretaker hobbled into the kitchen. "I figured I may as well be useful," she said.

He nodded. "Well, you're doing a mighty good job of

it. I'm sorry the place is such a mess. I don't get around like I used to."

"It's a big house for one person to maintain."

"Your stepfather wouldn't let no one on the property but me and that one man who ran errands for him—buying supplies and such. I don't suppose he liked people overly much."

"I don't suppose he did. I'm surprised William didn't hire someone to clean it after my stepfather passed."

"He tried. Had three different women come out here for the job, but they all left straightaways. All got spooked by the place. Three women talking about haunts and such was enough to keep all the rest away."

"Funny, William didn't mention any 'haunts and such' when he was proposing that I come live here for two weeks."

Amos rubbed his chin and nodded. "I expect William don't believe in haunts."

"Uh-huh." Neither had she until she came here. And now…now, she didn't know what she believed.

"Well, if you don't need anything from me," Amos said, "I got a toilet to fix on the backside of the house."

"I don't need anything, but thank you."

The grizzled old caretaker nodded and started to turn.

Before she could change her mind, Alaina said, "Amos, you knew my mother, right?"

"'Course. I was born here. Ain't ever lived anywhere else. Was here the night your mother was born and here the night she went away."

"What was she like? I have these flashes of memory, but they're so brief, and I…"

She what? Wanted to remember? She wasn't sure. If she remembered the good times, then it might make her even more sad and angry that they were so few. If she remembered the bad times, it might make her even more sad and angry that they were so many.

"She was beautiful," Amos said, "but I already told you as much. Thing was, with Ophelia, it wasn't just her outside. Her inside was just as pretty. She was smart and funny but most important, she was kind. She had a big heart, just like her momma and daddy."

Amos's eyes misted over as he talked about her mother and she felt a lump form in her throat, that the crotchety caretaker still missed the girl he'd known.

"Well, I best leave you to it," Amos said and left the kitchen.

Alaina watched him walk away and wondered how different everyone's life would have been if her mother had lived. It seemed everyone lost when her mother died.

Everyone except her stepfather.

Chapter Ten

Carter made the lonely drive to the estate and parked his truck behind Alaina's SUV. The evening sun cast an orange glow over the top of the swamp and onto the front of the house. His afternoon had been long and frustrating and the last thing he'd wanted to deal with was Alaina LeBeau. However, he'd made a promise to William and more important, his mother, and he wasn't about to go back on his word. Plus, he had to make her aware of the situation with Jack.

He knocked on the front door, expecting to have to pound on it next if Alaina was off in the depths of this monstrosity, but he was surprised when the door opened seconds later. Even more surprising was the smile she gave him.

"Hi, there," she said. "Come on in."

Technically, he'd just accomplished most everything he had to accomplish. Alaina was on property, giving her credit for her first full day of occupancy, but her chipper attitude roused his curiosity, so he stepped inside.

"I'm getting the kitchen in order," she said as they walked down the hall.

"You seem very cheerful for someone who's cleaning."

She laughed. "The day started off a little rocky, but I gave myself an attitude adjustment this afternoon. Now

I'm on a mission to restore the house to the place I remember. It really was beautiful at one time."

"I don't doubt it. My mom says your mother was a woman of infinite class and exquisite taste. She's never wrong about such things."

Alaina grinned at him. "I really must meet your mom sometime. I think I'd like her."

"Everyone does."

He stepped into the kitchen and drew up short. "Wow!"

The cherrywood cabinets gleamed as if a coat of gloss had been applied to them. The glass fronts were crystal clear, showing the neatly stacked china inside. The stone countertops were polished to a high sheen and the stainless steel appliances appeared as if they'd never been touched before. The cherrywood breakfast table had received the same treatment as the cabinets, and the old green cushions had been replaced with pale yellow that matched the paint that now covered one wall.

"You're painting?"

"The wallpaper was so dated, but it was stuck to the wall like glue. No use taking it off, so I'm covering it with primer and then painting over it."

"Let me just say again—wow. I can't believe you've done all this today."

Alaina looked pleased. "I've made three trips into Calais for supplies. I think Sam has a crush on me."

"I'm sure he does. He's a smart boy." Carter smiled. It was hard to stay aggravated in the presence of someone so happy and satisfied.

Alaina flushed a bit and opened the refrigerator. "Would you like a soda? Or how about a beer? Are you off work?"

"I am definitely off work and a beer would be great."

She pulled two bottles out of the refrigerator and passed

him one before sliding onto a bar stool. He sat on the stool next to her and took a big sip of the beer, then sighed with content.

"Long day?" Alaina asked.

"The longest. This town doesn't normally have much going on, but today tested the limits of my patience."

"Why? What happened?"

"Well, it started with Owen—the owner of the general store—swearing that he'd been robbed, but he couldn't produce a list of inventory or any proof at all that items were missing, other than he 'felt the stock was off.' Then the Boudreaux boys set their uncle's garage on fire with a soldering iron. By the time we got the fire out, Mr. and Mrs. Paulson—who are both ninety if they're a day—backed into each other in their driveway. Apparently, they both thought they were driving to visit their daughter and neither realized the other was in a completely different, *moving* car."

Alaina covered her mouth with her hand, but he could see the smile she was hiding.

"Then Marty Philippe ran his boat clean up his boat trailer and into the back of his buddy's truck when they were loading up for the day, and they got in a fight at the dock. I suspect beer was involved in that one, but by then, I was already too exhausted to care."

Alaina dropped her hand and burst out laughing.

He stared at her for a moment, then the hilarity of the situation and his delivery set in and he chuckled. "I guess that does sound rather ridiculous, especially if you're not used to small-town drama."

"You get used to this?"

He smiled. "Some people do."

"But not you?"

It was a question, but it came out more like a statement.

Carter took another sip of beer. Was he really that easy to read? Could everyone tell that he throttled himself every day to achieve such a slow pace?

"I suppose I got used to the speed things happened in the city," he said.

"I get that. And I'm guessing garage fires, senior driveway accidents and drunken boat loading didn't fall under the purview of the New Orleans Police Department."

"Not even close. On a good day, I had only three open murder cases on my desk."

"And on a bad day?"

He didn't want to think about the bad days. The bad days—one very awful day in particular—were the reason he'd finally turned in his badge and gun and headed back home. Even his mother didn't know what had delivered the final blow, and if he hadn't shared it with the one woman he could trust, he wasn't about to share it with one who was highly suspect.

"So what about you?" he asked, changing the subject.

"What about me?"

"I see how you spent most of your day. Was all of it without incident?"

"Sure," she said, a little too quickly.

He stared at her and she looked down at the counter. "You don't look sure."

She looked back up at him and blew out a breath. "I found a couple of things where they didn't belong. A folder last night and then my flash drive today."

"And you're sure you didn't move them?"

"Yes. At least, I think I'm sure."

She didn't sound very sure, but she did sound rattled, and that bothered him. "Did you ask Amos?"

"I didn't have to. He worked over here a bit this afternoon and took some time to show me around the downstairs. He apologized up front that none of the bedrooms had been cleaned. He said the arthritis in his knees was so bad he couldn't walk up the stairs. Both incidents occurred in the bedroom, so it couldn't have been him."

Carter frowned.

"What's wrong?" she asked.

"Nothing...at least, I hope it's nothing." He told her about his conversation with the cook.

"Oh, no," she said, clearly unhappy. "Is there anyone in this town that my stepfather didn't screw over?"

"You're not responsible for the things your stepfather did, and given that you and your sisters were screwed over more than anyone, I don't think anyone with a clue is holding things Purcell did against you."

"Maybe not, but I'm still glad the grill at the café is in plain sight. I'm guessing I won't be a favorite customer there."

"That's Jack's problem."

"So you say, but it seems a lot like it's mine. Like I need anything else to add to the list."

She blew out a breath, shaking her head.

"Is something else wrong?" he asked, getting the impression that he didn't know everything that was going on.

"There is one more thing—probably nothing—but I promised I'd keep you informed."

"Let me decide if it's nothing."

"My former boss called me today. Someone vandalized his car and left a note saying 'All of you will pay.'"

"And he thinks the note refers to you and him?"

"He doesn't know who it refers to, but given that I worked there, the police felt I should be told."

"Uh-huh." He studied her for a couple of seconds. It was clear to him that she was leaving something out. Maybe her boss didn't have any idea who'd left the note, but Alaina had someone in mind—someone she wasn't ready to share with him.

"You didn't get a call from him, by any chance?" she asked.

"No. Should I have?"

"Not necessarily. I got a call earlier from the firm's phone number, but my signal was too weak to answer. I thought maybe he was calling back with more information. I'd given him your name earlier and told him if he couldn't reach me to call you in case of an emergency."

"Nothing came through dispatch. Maybe he was just following up."

"Maybe."

"Did he say if the police want you to do anything in particular?"

"No. He just said they felt I should be informed of the incident and kept in the loop on the investigation."

He nodded. "They want you to be more aware and notice anything out of the norm in case you're a target."

"'Anything out of the norm'—that's funny."

"I know it will be harder to do outside of your element, even worse here."

"It's impossible here. Either I'm losing my mind, or something is happening in this house." She studied him for a second, as if trying to decide whether to continue, then she blurted out, "Do you believe in ghosts?"

"I… Well… What prompted this question?"

She sighed. "Cops and therapists. They always answer questions with a question."

"I'm sorry. I wasn't trying to be difficult, but the question caught me off guard."

"Yeah, it's not exactly normal fare for me either." She brushed a lock of hair away from her face and Carter could see her hand wasn't as steady as it had been when she'd handed him the beer. Something had spooked her. He'd wondered as much when he'd seen her in the café at the crack of dawn, but he'd dismissed it as being a morning person who'd slept poorly in a strange bed all night.

"Did you see something?" he asked quietly.

She stared at him for several seconds, biting her lower lip, then finally nodded. "Last night, I woke and something was floating above my bed. It looked almost like a human wearing a long, white robe, but I couldn't make out details because it was hazy, almost like smoke."

He placed his beer on the counter and leaned back.

"You think I'm crazy," she said. "I get it. I'd think I was crazy, too. It's just that—"

"No," he interrupted, "I don't think you're crazy, but I do find it interesting."

"Does that mean you believe in ghosts?"

"I don't know. Maybe?" He blew out a breath. "I mean, it seems there are more things in this world that are unexplained than are explained, so why not?"

"So you think I saw one?"

"I didn't say that."

She sighed. "You *do* think I'm crazy. I'm beginning to think so myself." She looked so distraught that he leaned forward and placed his hand on her arm.

"I don't think you're crazy. I think you're a normal woman in an extraordinary situation. You wouldn't be human if you weren't anxious."

"You think my mind and imagination are playing tricks on me?"

"It would be hard for them not to. I mean, this room looks nice now except for the overgrown rain forest outside the windows, but the house is far from inviting and it's strange to you because you were so young when you left."

"You mean when I was forced to leave?" Her jaw flexed with anger.

Carter gently squeezed her arm. "What Purcell did to you and your sisters was wrong. If karmic justice existed, he would have died a horrible death years ago. But this is what you got dealt."

"I never win at gambling."

"You will this time. You'll complete your stay and with any luck, come out of it ahead by one creepy house and two sisters. Hopefully, the sisters aren't creepy."

Her lips quivered for a second and then she smiled. "Why are you being so nice to me when I've been so abrupt with you?"

"I'm a nice guy."

She raised one eyebrow.

"And I'm very afraid of my mother."

ALAINA STOOD at the front door, watching Carter's tail-lights disappear into the swamp. He'd lingered over the beer and Alaina could tell he was hesitant to leave her here alone. She knew it would have taken only a simple request and he would have stayed, but what would that have accomplished?

The rest of her time in the house would still stretch before her, and Carter could hardly be expected to move in for the duration. He'd agreed to keep the terms of the will because of his mother's friendship with the attorney. He was under no obligation to do that, much less take on full-time security duties.

That's true, but that's not the real reason you wanted him to go.

She sighed as she closed the door and locked it. Damn the voices in her head. They were always right. If she was being one hundred percent honest, the thought of a ghost scared her far less than her attraction to the sheriff.

It was an attraction she was trying hard to fight but was losing ground. He was a hard man to ignore—a man who kept promises because he loved his mother, and who had a body and face that belonged in one of those Men in Uniform calendars.

Admit he's a god and get it over with.

"Fine. He's a god!" she yelled into the cavernous entry.

Her words bounced off the walls, echoing back at her. And then another followed them.

"I don't know that God talks to mortals anymore... least not out loud."

Alaina whirled around as Amos exited the hall to the laundry room and strode toward her.

"Amos! You gave me a bit of a scare."

The ancient caretaker shuffled across the marble floor, his arthritic knees making progress slow. "A woman who shouts at God shouldn't be startled so easily."

"No, I wasn't... I was... Never mind. What can I do for you, Amos?"

"Came over to bring you this." He held up a lantern. "It's probably old-fashioned to you, but it's a good source of light when the power goes out. Better than using a flashlight if you need to light up a room."

Alaina took the lantern from Amos. "Are we supposed to have another storm tonight?"

"Not tonight. Maybe tomorrow."

She let out the breath she'd been holding. All day, she'd been working herself up to sleeping in the bedroom, but the last thing she needed piling on was another storm and the loss of electricity. "That's good news."

Amos nodded and turned to leave.

"Wait… I… The other day, you said that my mother would come visit me."

"Yep." His delivery was matter-of-fact and his expression one of complete seriousness.

"You do know she's dead, right?" She watched him closely as soon as she delivered those words, hoping that she hadn't upset some great balance of denial.

"'Course I know that." Amos gave her an indignant look. "I'm old, not senile."

"Then how…"

He stared at her for several seconds, his brown eyes almost black in the dim light, wisps of silver hair that needed a trim and a comb stuck out in all directions. Her pulse ticked up just a bit and with every passing second of silence, she could feel it growing stronger—louder.

"I seen her myself," he said, his voice low and reverent. "Wouldna believed it if someone else had made the claim, but it's hard to deny what's right in front of you."

"You saw…" Her voice caught in her throat. "You saw my mother?"

Amos nodded. "The first time was right after she passed. The master took you all away and the house was empty. A storm was brewing and I came to make sure everything was closed tight. When I left you girls' room upstairs, I saw her walking toward me on the landing."

"Oh." Alaina covered her mouth with her hand. That was the same place she'd seen her mother in her memory earlier. "How did she look?"

"Sad. Like she was lost. As she got closer, I could see her lips moving like she was trying to tell me something, but I couldn't hear nothing."

Alaina frowned. The caretaker's experience was nothing like her memory. Her mother had looked happy and vibrant, but then in her memory, she'd been alive and about to spend time with her children. If ghosts really did exist, couldn't they be sad?

"I seen her several times since that one," Amos continued. "Always before a storm. Always sad and trying to speak to me. I wish I could hear her." Amos rubbed his eyes with his fingers and Alaina could see his eyes were misty.

"She was a good woman," he said, "just like her mother. I miss her every day."

"Oh, Amos." She felt the tears brimming in her eyes. "I miss her, too."

He gave her a single nod and stared at the floor as if sharing his feelings embarrassed him. "If she's gonna talk to anyone, I figure it will be one of you girls."

"I hope you're right."

"Well, if you don't need anything, I best be going before it gets dark."

"I'm fine. Thank you. Be careful walking home."

"Always am. Mystere Parish swamps ain't nothing to be casual about. Getting casual can get you stuffed in a pine box." He turned around and shuffled back toward the laundry room.

Stuffed in a pine box.

Alaina shook her head. The man had a way with words.

CARTER PACED HIS CABIN, not even glancing at the baseball game playing on television. Alaina's vandalism story bothered him for several reasons, but the main one was that he knew she was holding something back. She may not know who'd vandalized her former boss's car, but she had her suspicions, and she wasn't sharing them with him. Which meant something could be coming his way and he wasn't prepared.

It was time to do a little digging into Alaina LeBeau's past.

He grabbed a beer and carried his laptop to the breakfast table. The police database was probably a waste of time. Based on William's description, the law firm she'd worked for in Baton Rouge wouldn't have run the risk of employing a criminal, so Google was what he had to work with.

He logged on to the internet and typed her name into the search box. Unless a person had achieved some level of fame, it was rare to find much about them using a simple internet search. Social and professional networking websites were often the only places people had an online presence.

The screen refreshed with the search results and his eyes widened. Pages and pages of results on Alaina, and the headlines weren't good—Child Serial Rapist Goes Free, Legal System Fail, Death of Another Child by Acquitted Serial Rapist.

He grabbed his beer and took a big drink, then clicked on the first link and began to read. An hour later, he got up from the table, dumped out his now-warm beer and paced back and forth from the kitchen to the living room—all ten steps of it.

At best, he'd hoped to find a couple of leads—angry businessmen whose merger didn't go through, or a useless son who didn't inherit as expected—but he hadn't expected to find that Alaina had been the lead defense attorney in such a sordid case. A case where winning had been the worst thing possible.

Her client, a seventeen-year-old boy accused of indecency with a child, had gone free, the jury acquitting him of all charges. Two weeks later, he'd attacked and murdered a six-year-old girl, this time the entire thing caught by a security camera. Techniques in the murder matched those used in the molestation of other children and two other murders he hadn't been linked to before this one. Details about the techniques that had never been released by the police.

No doubt existed this time. The boy was responsible for this attack and murder and had been for all the others. By doing a great job, Alaina had helped set a child killer free.

He stopped pacing and stared out the window into the pitch-black swamp. What the hell had she been doing as lead on a case like that? William told him she worked civil and business cases. He'd never mentioned criminal work and couldn't have known about this case or he would have told him up front.

The entire thing stank to high heaven.

Suddenly, he remembered a guy he'd met at a law enforcement conference in Baton Rouge the year before. He was a state prosecutor and had given Carter his card with his cell number in case he was ever in town. Carter opened a kitchen drawer and pulled out a stack of business cards. Finally, he located the right one and grabbed his cell phone.

The prosecutor, Rob, answered on the second ring. "Carter Trahan. Are you in town and looking for a good time?"

"I wish. Unfortunately, I'm hard at work."

"I thought you chucked NOLA and moved to some bayou town with ten people and a hundred gators? Don't tell me you've run into a hotbed of crime."

"Just a single problem," Carter replied, "but with the potential to be red-hot."

"Sounds intriguing. I'm assuming you didn't call me to shoot the breeze, so how can I help?"

"A woman returned here recently to settle her mother's estate. The will is strange and requires her to stay here for a bit. She was an attorney in Baton Rouge and there's the off chance that trouble from one of her cases might follow her here."

"Who's the attorney?"

"Alaina LeBeau."

Rob whistled. "That was one screwed-up mess that I thank God every day I had no part in. There's no shortage of news coverage on that case, so I assume you're not calling me about anything you can find online?"

"No. I read the reports and they seem straightforward as do the facts."

"But?"

"But there's something that doesn't make sense to me. I can't find another reference to Alaina LeBeau handling criminal cases."

"She hasn't," Rob confirmed.

"Then why make her lead on something this big?"

"I can tell you what I suspect, but you're probably not going to like it."

Carter sighed. "She was scapegoated."

"You got it. The case had stench all over it, but word is the father of the killer—a state senator—is a longtime friend of the partners of the law firm Alaina worked for. The only reason to put a junior attorney with zero experience in criminal proceedings as the lead is so she'd be available to take the fall if things went south."

"And this went so far south it's renting space in Antarctica."

"You got it. So what exactly got you calling me at 10:00 p.m. on a Friday night? I know it's not general curiosity."

Carter repeated what Alaina had told him about the vandalism.

"And the police think it has something to do with the case?" Rob asked.

"She says the police aren't committing to anything, but they felt she should be informed just in case."

"Standard covering-your-butt stuff. So again, what's got *you* calling me at 10:00 p.m.?"

Carter smiled. "You must be hell in a courtroom."

"Only if you're a bad guy or a defense attorney."

"Fair enough. The truth is, I have a bad feeling about it. I can't put my finger on why, but ever since Alaina arrived in town, something has felt off. And now you're probably regretting ever giving your phone number to a delusional person."

"Not in the least. Look, I've spent more hours than I can count working with cops. The best ones have this sixth sense about things. I don't know how to explain it—certainly, there's no scientific explanation—but I've seen it firsthand. If your instincts are telling you that trouble is coming, I recommend you be on the lookout."

"Thanks, Rob."

"No problem. Give me a call next time you're in Baton Rouge."

"You got it." Carter disconnected the call. He understood completely why Alaina had dodged his question on suspects. She was probably still mortified, and if he'd pegged her properly, felt guilty and responsible.

He ran one hand through his hair, his emotional side and logical side waging a war. Logically, he knew the only person responsible for horrid acts was the person committing them, but that was a very black-and-white view of life. The reality was, he believed all sorts of things contributed to something taking place. Life was more often many shades of gray.

His emotional side argued that if high-end attorneys didn't do such a good job defending the guilty, more of them would be in prison where they belonged instead of back out on the streets with innocents at their mercy. That argument and one too many run-ins with shady defense attorneys were the final straws in Carter's calling it quits with the NOLA Police Department and heading home.

Now he had his worst nightmare in his lap. A defense attorney who'd successfully freed a monster, and it was his job to protect her from her own actions.

William owed him huge for this. Huge.

Chapter Eleven

Alaina's arms ached as she dried off her tired body. Apparently, all those hours spent at the gym didn't prepare one for painting and Olympic-level cleaning. On the plus side, she'd made significant progress with the kitchen and was very pleased with the result. Only the overgrown shrubbery outside the kitchen windows put a damper on the cheerful room. First thing tomorrow, she was going to ask Amos if he had some tools to help her tackle the brush. It wouldn't be the most professional job, but she could at least clear some of it away to allow in more sunshine.

She pulled on her sleeping wear and slipped into flip-flops, thinking she'd tackle some upstairs floors tomorrow so she could actually go barefoot, a habit her adoptive mother always griped about, but one she was never able to shed. Her long hair was dripping wet in the humidity, but a towel dry was all it was getting. Then it went on top of her head, held there with a clip. It was going in a ponytail again tomorrow anyway.

She hung the towel over the shower rod and left the bathroom, ready to collapse in bed. Before she'd taken three steps on the landing, the lights in the entry downstairs clicked off. She froze, listening for the sound of someone moving downstairs, but only silence greeted her.

Glancing down the hallway, she saw the lamp next to her bed still glowing. It wasn't a power outage.

She slipped off her flip-flops and hurried to her room to grab her cell phone.

No signal.

She held in a stream of cursing, angry once again at her vulnerable state. When her mother had drafted her strange inheritance requirements, she'd had no idea what position she'd be putting her children in.

The squeaking of a door hinge downstairs had her reaching for her pistol and car keys. Time to get out of the house and get help. Peering out the patio doors, she bit her lip. She'd told Carter she had no problem springing over the balcony and running, and that much was true, but an inspection of the kitchen courtyard that morning had revealed massive thornbushes directly below the balcony. Jumping now could cause more injuries than she could run with.

She shoved her cell phone and keys in her yoga pants pockets and mentally reviewed her plan. All she had to do was hurry downstairs and out the front door. If she couldn't see the intruder in the dark, then he couldn't see her either, and she'd remain barefoot to mask her steps. Gripping her pistol with both hands, she slipped out of the bedroom and down the hallway.

The dim light from the lamp faded away as she inched down the hallway. By the time she reached the top of the stairwell, she had only enough light to make out the first few steps. She released the pistol with one hand and placed it on the railing as she slid her foot forward to take the first step down.

She must have miscalculated, or lost her balance, because the next thing she knew, she was lurching forward onto the stairs, then tumbling over and over, her limbs banging against the hard marble. She yelled out both in pain and terror, then her head slammed against one of the iron balusters and everything went black.

CARTER JOGGED as fast as possible down the overgrown path through the swamp to Amos's cabin. He'd been calling Alaina since early this morning, but she'd never answered or returned any of his calls and text messages. He'd waited a couple of hours, thinking she might be sleeping in after all the work she'd done in the kitchen, but when the morning approached ten o'clock and she still hadn't contacted him, he'd driven to the house.

Her car was in the driveway, but pounding on the front door hadn't brought any response. Even worse, when he'd dialed her number again, he could swear he heard the faint ring of her cell phone on the other side of the door. He'd hurried around back, remembering Alaina mentioning the day before that she wanted to remove some of the brush from the kitchen patio, but it was clear she hadn't started work there yet.

That was when he'd decided she might have gone to see Amos for tools, and took off for the caretaker's cabin, trying to remain calm. Alaina was under no obligation to tell him or anyone else her every move, especially if she did all her moving in Calais. Nor was she required to be strapped to her cell phone, and even if she was, it was still her choice to take calls. Maybe she was busy and didn't want to be bothered. When he was working on a project at his cabin, he tended to ignore the outside world in favor of speed and efficiency.

Amos was just exiting the toolshed when Carter stepped out of the overgrown trail and into the clearing where the caretaker's quarters stood. Carter called out a greeting and Amos looked at him and frowned.

"Carter? What are you doing all the way out here? Aren't you on duty?"

"I'm looking for Alaina. Have you seen her?"

Amos shook his head. "Not since last night. She's not at the big house?"

"Her car is there, but she's not answering." Carter's pulse quickened. "I need your key."

The caretaker's eyes widened and he pulled the keys from his pocket and indicated a black iron one to Carter. "That's the one. I'll be along behind you."

Carter took the key and broke out in a run up the trail, cursing at himself as he went. The dead brush scratched his bare forearms, but he didn't slow. He'd had a feeling something was wrong that morning. Why hadn't he driven out here right away? His mother had told him not to ignore things like this and he'd gone and done it anyway. If something had happened to Alaina, he'd never forgive himself.

He burst out of the trail and into the courtyard, then skidded to a stop in front of the doors. The massive iron key turned easily and he pushed the door open and ran inside, yelling for Alaina. His voice echoing off the vaulted ceiling was the only sound that greeted him. He started to turn toward the kitchen, when he heard a groan coming from the stairwell.

He rushed up the stairs and found Alaina crumpled in a ball midway up the giant circular staircase. Her hand covered the side of her head and dried blood covered her fingers.

"Alaina!" He dropped to his knees and checked her pulse, then blew out a breath of relief when the strong heartbeat pounded against his fingers. Gently tapping her cheek with his fingers, he called her name.

She groaned again and slowly opened her eyes. When

her eyes locked on Carter, she lurched upward, then clutched her head with both hands and sank back down, closing her eyes again.

"Don't move," he told her. "You've cracked your head. At best, you'll be dizzy and nauseous. At worst, you've got a concussion."

"What are you doing here in the middle of the night?" she asked.

Carter's heart clutched. The dried blood had been a clear indicator that the accident hadn't happened recently, but the fact that she'd been unconscious all night was definitely cause for concern.

"It's not the middle of the night. It's almost 11:00 a.m. What time did you fall?"

She pushed herself up, slowly this time, and he put his hands behind her back to help her to an upright position.

"Around midnight," she said.

He lifted a piece of her matted hair away to get a better look at her head, then blew out a breath of relief at the small gash. "It doesn't look deep, but I need to get you to the doctor. You've been unconscious a long time. How did this happen?"

She stared blankly at him for a moment. "I took a shower, then left the bathroom… Oh, I remember! I heard something downstairs."

"What did you hear?"

"It sounded like squeaky hinges from a door, then all the downstairs lights went off, but the power was still on. So I grabbed my keys and gun and was going to sneak downstairs and go get you."

He looked down at her bare feet. "And you slipped on the landing."

"I guess so." She frowned. "I don't really remember how it happened. I just remember falling over and over and then everything went black. I'm usually not that clumsy."

"You're not used to your surroundings and it was dark." He made excuses, not wanting to stress her any further if it was a simple case of ill balance. "Let's get you to the doctor."

He rose and she started to follow, but he put a hand on her shoulder. "You don't need to walk, especially down stairs." He leaned over and scooped her up from the stairs.

Her eyes widened in surprise, but she wrapped her arms around him for balance and didn't protest. Her head probably hurt more than she was willing to admit. As he stepped off the stairs, Amos walked through the front door.

The caretaker took one look at Alaina and paled. "Are you all right, miss?"

"She fell down the stairs late last night," Carter explained as he carried her outside. Amos hurried beside him and opened his truck door. "She's got a good crack on her head and has been unconscious all night. I'm going to take her to Doc Broussard."

Amos nodded. "That's good," he said as Carter gently placed Alaina on the passenger's seat. "You go take care of yourself, miss. I'll watch the house."

Carter jumped into the truck and pulled slowly away from the house, making every attempt to avoid the biggest holes on the dirt road.

"Someone was in the house with me," Alaina said, her voice wavering. "Why is someone trying to scare me?"

Carter clenched his jaw. "I don't know, but I'm damn well going to find out."

Doc Broussard was a silver-haired gentleman who had probably been quite a ladies' man in his day. He charmed

Alaina with his gentle touch and calm concern. Carter was the complete opposite. He stood in the corner of the room and she could practically feel the tension coming off him. Carter was definitely concerned, but it was anything but calm.

Doc Broussard lowered the X-ray he'd been studying and smiled at her. "Everything looks fine. You got a good crack, but I don't see any swelling or blood pools."

Her back and neck loosened a bit at his words, some of the tension releasing. "That's great news. It worried me that I'd been unconscious for so long."

Doc Broussard nodded. "It's not optimal for those with a head injury to sleep, but it doesn't appear as if there's any damage done here. But if you start experiencing bad headaches or nausea, you need to let me know. I can schedule you an MRI in New Orleans."

"Let's hope it doesn't come to that."

"Perhaps… Well… I know it's none of my business," Doc Broussard said, "but maybe you shouldn't be staying in that big house. Amos hasn't been able to keep it up for years. The thing is probably a death trap."

"It's not bad," Alaina assured him. "It's more dirty than anything, and unfortunately, I have to stay there to meet the terms of my mother's will—at least for two weeks."

Doc Broussard frowned. "I'd heard the rumors about that tomfoolery. I'd hoped they were exaggerated, but apparently they're not. You'd think William could have found a way around such nonsense."

"He tried," Alaina said. "He's no happier about the situation than me or you."

Carter coughed and Alaina glanced over at him.

"He may *even* be as unhappy as Carter, who's tasked with ensuring I am in residence every day of the two weeks," she said, trying not to smile.

Doc Broussard shot a look at Carter and grinned. "What's wrong with you, boy? Keeping watch over a beautiful woman seems the best job in town. Or are you afraid your mother will find out the young lady got injured on your watch?"

Alaina's smile broke through at the look of utter dismay on Carter's face. "I really must meet your mother."

Doc Broussard nodded. "Willamina Trahan is a force to be reckoned with. Beautiful and smart. If I was a braver man, I would ask her out, but as it is, I'll just have to settle for a nice glass of wine and Netflix."

"Are we done here?" Carter asked, clearly uncomfortable with the doctor's dating comment.

"Absolutely." Doc Broussard pulled a card from his pocket and handed it to Alaina. "If you have any questions or concerns, call me immediately. That's my cell number and I try to keep it on me at all times."

Alaina took the card and placed it in her pocket. "Thanks," she said and eased off the table, careful not to jostle her slightly aching head.

"Warm water on the cut a couple of times a day," Doc Broussard said as he walked them out. "I don't think it needs a stitch, but if it doesn't start healing in a day or two, come back and see me and we'll reassess."

"Thank you." Alaina gave him a parting wave as she eased past Carter, who was holding the door open for her.

Carter was silent as he helped her into his truck, and the lack of conversation continued as he drove down Main Street. He looked pensive and slightly frustrated and she had to wonder if he was really so humorless that a little harmless joking put him in a foul mood.

"He's right, you know," Carter finally said, breaking the silence.

"About what?"

"You shouldn't be staying in that house—at least not alone."

Alaina shrugged, trying to maintain her cool, even though the thought of another night alone in that house was beginning to worry her already-frayed nerves. "Like I said before, no other options."

"To staying in the house, no. But I'm going to fix the alone part."

She shook her head. "Even if you could get him to do it, I don't think Amos would be much protection."

"I'm not talking about Amos. I'm talking about me."

"Oh, no!" All sorts of potential scenes flashed through Alaina's mind and her lack of clothing was a common theme. "I can't ask you to do that. It's not your responsibility. None of this is."

"You're not asking and I'm not offering. I'm telling you. Either I stay there until I can figure out what's going on or I tell William to remove you from the house. You already narrowly missed a serious head injury. I'm not about to have worse on my conscience."

One look at his set jaw and determined expression and Alaina knew it was futile to argue. If the estate attorney thought she was in imminent danger, she had no doubt he'd pull her out of the house until his concerns were alleviated.

"Wow," she grumbled. "You really are afraid of your mother."

He looked over at her and grinned. "Think you're funny, don't you?" He pressed the accelerator, but instead of turning right toward the estate, he turned left.

"Where are you going?"

"Because you want to meet my mother so badly, I figure there's no time like the present. While you two think up a million ways to 'fix' my life, I'll go check out the house."

Alaina stared at him. "You can't just foist me off un- announced on your mother. That's rude, Carter. Maybe you do need fixing."

"Rude? Are you kidding me? My mom has been dying to meet you since before you got here, and she'll be thrilled to be the one to fuss over you in your time of need. She's a big caretaker, my mom. Your visiting would actually be doing her a favor."

She sighed. "Small towns are very odd."

"You have no idea."

WILLAMINA TRAHAN, as predicted, was thrilled to meet Alaina and horrified to hear about her fall. She immedi- ately put her arm around Alaina's shoulders and drew her into the kitchen where she insisted on making coffee and cutting her a piece of apple pie. The apple pie looked deli- cious enough that Carter was tempted to linger, but curi- osity won out and he left his mother's house and headed to the estate.

Amos's key was still in his pocket, so gaining entry into the house was no problem. He yelled out as he walked through the front doors in case the caretaker was some- where inside, but only silence greeted him.

He glanced at the downstairs entry lights, all of which seemed to be in fine working order now. The second thing he intended to do was look for a short, but that was only if the first thing he intended to do turned up nothing. The first thing he was going to do was try to determine how exactly Alaina had fallen.

Certainly, if she was spooked, in the dark, in an un- familiar place, she could have lost her balance or taken a wrong step, and that was exactly what he'd told her. But he wanted to make sure another reason wasn't behind her sudden clumsy spell. He took the stairs two steps at a time until he reached the second floor. On the landing, he crouched down to study the bottom of the newels, running his fingers lightly up the base on each side of the stairs.

His pulse spiked a bit when he felt the tiny indentions that circled near the bottom of each newel. Someone had strung wire across the steps when Alaina was showering, then turned off the entry lights to prompt her to come downstairs in the dark. He'd bet money on it. The question was who?

Aside from Jack, it seemed unlikely that someone in Calais had a problem with Alaina unless it had something to do with the will. It was time for a conversation with William to determine who benefited if Alaina and her sisters didn't inherit. Of course, that only mattered if the secondary beneficiaries were even aware of their status, which he doubted, as even the sisters had not been aware of the terms of their mother's will until after Purcell's death.

It was far more likely that it was personal—that someone from Alaina's past had followed her to Calais and was using the remote location and her solitary living arrangement as an opportunity to scare her. But the wire was far more than a prank. Alaina could have easily been killed.

He headed downstairs to check the lights but already knew he'd find nothing wrong with them. Bad wiring hadn't rigged a trip wire on the stairs, nor did he think it was a coincidence that the lights went off exactly as Alaina exited the bathroom. Someone was toying with her.

As soon as he finished here, he'd head back to his mother's. Being the consummate hostess—and being his mother—she'd insist on their staying for dinner. But as soon as it was over and he'd grabbed a change of clothes from his cabin, he and Alaina were going to have a long talk about the people who may want her dead—starting with everyone related to the one case she was probably trying to forget.

WILLAMINA, WHO'D INSISTED Alaina call her Willa, had been the consummate host. Alaina smiled at her as she carried a tray of iced tea onto the spacious stone patio behind her house. It was warm and humid, but Willa had assured her that her swamp cooler would make the atmosphere pleasant and allow them to see the sunset over the swamp, something the older woman said she enjoyed most evenings.

Alaina hadn't been convinced that anything could best the heat and humidity of Louisiana in the summer, but she'd been intrigued by the term *swamp cooler* and couldn't resist heading outside to see what one looked like.

It had turned out to be a giant water-cooled fan that seemed to lower the temperature on the patio by a good twenty degrees, which was impressive. She suspected the loud whirling wouldn't be accepted at her condo back in Baton Rouge, but then, she wasn't even certain she'd return there except to pack. Maybe when all this was over, she'd find a small town to move to. This one was rather charming and if all small towns had women as nice and interesting as Willa, who could bake pie like an angel, it would be all that more tempting.

Maybe you should just stay here.

The thought flashed through her mind and she froze. Where in the world had that come from? Calais was lovely in its own way, but she could hardly hope to have a legal career here. Any town could support a doctor or dentist, but few small places had enough need for an attorney to support them. Not to mention that while Alaina was enjoying the slower pace for the moment, she knew it wasn't something she could adjust to on a daily basis. She had to have enough mental stimulation keeping her busy or she'd get restless, bored and unhappy.

Willa handed her a glass of tea and motioned to patio chairs placed directly in the path of the swamp cooler airflow. She took a seat and sipped the tea, then sighed, savoring the sweet, crisp taste.

"I don't usually drink sweetened tea," Alaina said, "but then, I never get tea that tastes like this in Baton Rouge either."

Willa nodded and took the seat across from her. "The secret is in steeping the tea. No cheating with coffee-pots and such. You either boil the water or set it out on a hot day on your porch. When it's just the right shade of brown, you add sugar and cold water and stick it in the refrigerator to chill."

Alaina didn't even want to think about exactly how many cups of sugar were in the tea. She was enjoying herself far too much and, quite frankly, deserved a bit of a treat. "Well, it tastes wonderful."

Willa smiled. "It's nice to see a young woman who isn't afraid to have a bit of sugar. Why, my niece took a swig of tea last time she was visiting and I thought she'd have apoplexy. Said it would put her over her calorie limit for the day. When I have to count the calories in my tea, I want to just pass on over to the big house. I bet there's no unsweetened tea in heaven."

Alaina laughed. "I hope you're right."

Willa studied her for a moment. "You're not what I expected."

"Really? What were you expecting?"

"Someone beautiful and I got that part right. Your mother was beautiful and you look a lot like her."

Alaina felt a flush rise up her neck at the compliment. "Thank you."

"I can't find any polite way of saying the rest, so I'll just come out with it—I expected you to be a taskmistress."

"Oh!" Alaina grinned. "There are some attorneys who would definitely support such a belief. So where did you get that idea—from Carter?"

Willa waved a hand in dismissal. "It's no secret that Carter's annoyed by this whole mess. It is rather a strange way to settle an estate, and I know there was no love lost between him and attorneys from his time spent in New Orleans. But I guess I thought you'd be rigid and humorless because William said you worked for the best firm in Baton Rouge. I figured if a young, beautiful woman was that successful, especially given the good ol' boy network, that she must be a taskmistress."

"I suppose there's a lot of truth to that. You have to be very focused and driven to make a play in my field, especially in a male-dominated firm, and most of the oldest and most prestigious are."

"But, dear, why would you want to pretend to be someone you're not? You're a bright, warm, interesting girl—why hide all that just to impress a bunch of men who probably aren't worth the time anyway? You should concentrate on finding something to do that utilizes your skill and education but that allows *you* to be *you*."

Alaina's eyes began to mist and she swallowed, trying to get rid of the lump in her throat. It was exactly the sort of thing she imagined a mother might say to her daughter. She needed to reply, but was afraid that if she opened her mouth, she'd start crying.

"Oh, no!" Willa said. "I've upset you."

"No," Alaina said, finally finding her voice. "I'm just…

I guess I'm not used to people looking past what I do and actually seeing me, much less caring that I'm happy with my life. It's a little overwhelming and sad, all at the same time. I mean, my adoptive parents took care of me, but I never felt a real part of their family."

Willa reached over to pat her knee. "You're a wonderful girl, Alaina, but you're going to have to tear down that wall you've built around you so that others can see. Not everyone is as perceptive as I am." She grinned.

Alaina smiled. "No, you're definitely one of a kind."

"Don't go telling her that." Carter's voice sounded behind her and Alaina jumped, then twisted her head around as he walked out onto the patio. He leaned over to kiss his mom on the forehead. "She already thinks she's got mythical magical powers."

Willa looked up at her son and sighed. "I don't know how I managed to bring such an unimaginative man into this world," she said, but Alaina could tell she was joking.

Carter smiled and pulled a chair up to join them. Alaina fidgeted a bit, wondering if Carter was going to talk about her situation in front of his mother. Willa had already insisted that she and Carter stay for dinner after he returned, and Alaina wasn't sure she could sit through an entire meal wondering what he'd found, if anything.

"I figure Mom's insisted on dinner," he said, "so I'll get the bad part out of the way."

Alaina let out a breath of relief. "Oh, good. I mean, not good that it's bad, but good that you're getting it out of the way."

"What did you find, Carter?" Willa asked.

"There was nothing wrong with the lights. Someone strung wire across the stair newel posts and then turned off the lights to draw you downstairs. They intended for you to fall—no question about it."

Alaina sucked in a breath. "Oh, no! But how? No one is supposed to have access to the house but myself, Amos and William."

"Other keys could be floating around," Carter said. "Those locks are old and probably haven't ever been changed."

"But you're going to do that, right?" Willa asked.

"Of course," Carter assured her, "but it's an old mansion with secret passageways stuck in the middle of a swamp that's swallowed it up. We have to assume there are other ways in besides the obvious."

Alaina bit her lip, her mind spinning with all the implications of Carter's finding. "Would Amos know about secret entries?"

"Maybe. He wasn't at home when I left the house, but as soon as I get a chance, I plan to quiz him on it."

"And in the meantime," Willa said, "you're not letting her stay there alone, right?"

"Absolutely not," Carter said. "I'll pack a bag after dinner and take one of the upstairs rooms until we can figure this all out."

Willa nodded and rose from her chair. "Then I best get the roast out and get you served. You've got a full night ahead of you."

Alaina watched as Willa walked into the house, closing the patio door behind her. "Why is this happening?"

"I don't know, but when we get to the house, you and I are going to have a serious discussion about potential suspects. I know you've been skirting around things since you got here, and I haven't pushed because we all have things we'd rather not discuss. But we're now past being polite. This is serious business."

"I know." She stared past him at the sun setting over the swamp. Here, in the cool breeze of the swamp cooler, with a glass of wonderful tea in her hand and a glorious sunset in front of her, she had been able to push the situation back far enough in her mind to slip into a moment of peace.

That moment was over.

Chapter Twelve

"Stay in my truck," Carter said, "but move over to the driver's seat. If I'm not back here in five minutes, then leave and go straight to the sheriff's office for help."

Alaina stared at Carter. "You can't go in there by yourself."

"You have the last two nights. It's actually my job to protect the citizens of this town, and for the time being, that includes you. So wait."

He jumped out of the truck, swinging the door shut behind him. Alaina watched as he walked in front of the vehicle, a grim look on his face. She waited until he disappeared inside the house, then slid over to the driver's seat and clutched the steering wheel.

She tried counting to one hundred, then singing a song, but finally gave up and looked at her watch. Only two minutes had passed. She blew out a breath of relief. It had seemed like so much longer, and the absolute last thing she wanted to do was drive away and leave Carter inside the house with God knew what or who.

As the seconds ticked by and the front door remained closed, her anxiety grew. What if he didn't come out before the five minutes were up? Would she be able to follow orders and drive away? She pulled her cell phone from her purse and cursed when she saw the no-service indicator.

Taking a deep breath, she looked at her watch again. Five more seconds. Four. Three. Two. One.

She gave the door one final look before starting the truck and putting it in gear. But before she pressed the accelerator, Carter hurried outside and pulled open the driver's door.

"Well?" she asked, her foot still hovering over the accelerator.

"It appears okay. I'll make a more thorough inspection once we're secured inside."

Alaina shut off the truck engine and followed Carter inside, mulling over the duplicity of "secured inside." As things stood, she wasn't sure she'd ever feel secure inside this house.

Carter tossed his duffel bag on the floor in the entry as soon as they walked inside, then turned to her. "First thing, I'm changing the door locks on the back door and the patio off the kitchen. The front door hardware is so old we'll probably have to special-order it."

Alaina nodded. "Let's hope there are only a couple of keys to it. They are these huge iron things. Surely there aren't that many."

"I hope that's the case. While I'm working on the laundry room exit, I want you to start inspecting all the rooms off the entry. Don't go down any of the hallways or upstairs. I want you easily within yelling distance."

"What am I looking for?"

"Any viable way to enter the house from the outside or to move through the house undetected. Servants' passageways, windows that don't lock—that sort of thing."

She started to head across the entry but paused and dug her pistol out of her purse. "Just in case," she said.

Carter gave her a single nod but didn't seem remotely fazed that she was going to prowl around with a loaded weapon. It gave her a moment of pause that he felt the situation was serious enough to merit it, but she put her purse on the entry table and headed to the first room to begin her search.

The room was a bit on the small side, and Alaina couldn't remember what it had been used for when she was a child. Now only two pieces of lonely furniture and a couple of boxes sat inside. She checked the windows, but both were nailed shut, with a thick coat of paint covering the nail heads. No one was coming in that way. The interior walls had peeling wallpaper, which would have easily shown a secret passageway.

The second room had become a haven for cardboard boxes, most of which had seen better days. She didn't bother attempting to check behind the wall of boxes on the far side. Even if a passageway was located behind them, no one was coming through it without crashing through a stack of cardboard.

She moved from that room to the next and then the one after that, repeating the process as she made her way around all the rooms off the first-floor entry. The sound of Carter working on the door lock was reassuring. If something happened, he was only a dash away. But as the minutes passed into an hour and all she came up with was dust and evidence of some small four-legged creatures that she did not want to personally encounter, she began to get more frustrated than nervous.

Someone had been in the house with her—they knew it for certain—but what if they'd simply used a key and entered through the front or back doors? Maybe all this looking for secret passageways was a waste of time. Certainly, servants' passages existed in the house as evidenced by the two Carter had already found, but those passages were used to move without being seen within a house, not from outside the house to inside of it and vice versa. If all the windows were locked and with new locks on the doors, surely whoever had managed to get in last night would no longer be able to terrorize her.

Unless they had a key to the front door.

No. She shook her head, putting that thought out of her mind, determined to believe that she'd be safe in the house from this point forward. Two weeks was nothing. She could manage two weeks of dust with ease.

She walked over to a window in the last room she had to check and stared out into the swamp that had swallowed up the massive backyard of the estate. In some ways, it was beautiful—all the layers of color and texture—but in other ways, it was cruel, overrunning everything in its path and swallowing it up until only remnants of the past remained.

The trailing, grasping vines bothered her more than she was willing to admit—made her feel claustrophobic as they pressed forward to consume the home. They felt alive somehow—not in the traditional way that they were alive—but alive and with a mind, as if they had a purpose and a plan for their progression.

"How's it going?"

Carter's voice sounded behind her and she whirled around. "Oh!"

"Sorry, I didn't mean to startle you," he said as he stepped into the room.

"No, it's my fault for not paying better attention."

He glanced out the window, then studied her for a couple of seconds. "You seemed engrossed with whatever you were looking at."

She glanced out the window and tried to think of something sane to say as the thoughts that had been rolling through her mind did not sound remotely rational. "I was…uh…"

"It's mesmerizing in a somewhat sinister way," he said quietly. "The swamp, that is."

She stared at him, dumbfounded. He'd captured her exact feeling so accurately, but never had she imagined that her fanciful thoughts would be shared by anyone else in Calais, especially Carter.

"I…I thought I was the only one…"

"Who felt the pull of the swamp?" Carter stepped next to her and looked out the window. "You're not."

She turned to look outside with him. "I guess I never figured you for the sort of person to believe in strange feelings." She blew out a breath. "I'm not explaining myself well."

"You don't have to. It's an uneasiness but with no obvious reason. Take right now, for instance—you should be more worried about what's going on inside the house, but I'm guessing you're more comfortable with the thought of sleeping inside tonight than walking across what used to be the back lawn in broad daylight."

"Yes, that's it exactly. But surely, you're not afraid to walk through the swamp. You grew up here."

He nodded. "I think it's because I grew up here that I'm willing to accept that the swamps of Mystere Parish are not the same as other swamps. There are so many stories about the strange happenings in Mystere that it's become impossible to separate truth from lore, but I imagine there's truth in most every story."

Despite the heat and humidity, a chill came over Alaina and she crossed her arms. "Voodoo stuff, I guess?" Rationally, she didn't believe in voodoo as a force of its own—only as something that worked off the power of belief of the supposedly cursed—but whatever she'd seen hovering over her bed that first night was no voodoo curse.

"I'm done with the locks," he said.

His voice broke into her fanciful thoughts, and she suddenly realized how close he stood to her. The bare skin of his arm scarcely brushed against her own bare skin and she could feel the heat coming off him. He was tall, but so was she, so their heads were only inches apart. She turned to look at him and found him looking directly at her. His jawline was covered with the shadow of emerging hair, making his chiseled cheeks and green eyes even more defined.

A rush of heat that had nothing to do with the humidity came over her, completely eclipsing her earlier chill. It would be so easy to lean in and press her lips to his. Despite his dislike of attorneys and his protests that he was only involved in her inheritance requirements because of his mother, she could tell he was attracted to her. It was in the way he looked at her when he thought she couldn't see—the way he took care to avoid being near her, as if he didn't trust himself.

Until now.

Her breath caught in her throat. Was he standing so close to her now because she'd been unnerved earlier and he was trying to comfort her, or was he feeling the pull to her the same as she was to him?

As if reading her mind, he took a step back and turned. "Let's do a quick check of the upstairs," he said. "We can do a more thorough search for passageways tomorrow. If he can't get in, he can't move around."

Alaina nodded and Carter left the room. Had he felt it, as well? Or was she imagining that he felt more for her than he showed? It wouldn't be the first time she'd thought a guy was interested in her only to find out he had a completely different agenda. Staring out the window again, she blew out a breath.

None of it mattered. At the end of two weeks, she was leaving Calais. Either way, the end was the same.

Always the same.

IN THE BEDROOM next to Alaina's, Carter carefully pulled the dusty sheet from the bed and rolled it up into a ball, trying to avoid scattering more dust all over the room. Being a typical man, it hadn't occurred to him to bring clean sheets with him, but fortunately, Alaina had gone through them all the day before, selecting the most worn for drop cloths and washing the rest in anticipation of her sisters' stay.

The shower in the bathroom a couple of doors down came on, the spray clinking against the porcelain tub. Immediately, a vision of Alaina standing naked under that stream of water flashed in front of him, as vivid as a movie and much more stimulating than any Hollywood actress he'd ever seen.

He unfolded the clean sheet and flipped it over the bed, trying to distract his mind from dangerous thoughts. Alaina was beautiful and sexy, but she was also an attorney and an outsider. When her time in Calais was done, she'd move on to conquer the legal world, and he'd still be right here, standing in her dust.

So have a fling. It's not like you haven't done it before.

A valid argument, albeit likely spurred along by parts of his body other than his mind, but this time it was different. Alaina was at a crossroads with her personal life and her career when she'd come to Calais. Now her life was in danger. To make a move on her right now would be grossly unfair, given that she couldn't possibly be thinking completely rationally.

A fling was fine as long as both parties were on the same page before getting started. But given the current situation, he was afraid that Alaina wasn't capable of being on the same page. The last thing he wanted to do was add more negatives about Calais to the long list she already carted around with her.

He finished making the bed, then headed to Alaina's bedroom to do a thorough search. The patio doors were secure and all the windows were locked. He ran his hands along all the walls, inspecting every inch, but didn't see any place where an opening could exist. The closet was stacked high with boxes, so even if there was a passageway that led into the tiny space, it wasn't accessible.

The room was secure, but he still wasn't happy about it. If he could get away with it, he'd drag his mattress in here and sleep in the same room, but he knew Alaina would balk at the suggestion. And it was just as well because the risk to their emotions might be higher than danger to Alaina's person.

As he closed the closet door, his cell phone rang. Rob. He frowned as he answered the call, already knowing that the attorney hadn't called him at 11:00 p.m. just to chat, especially given their last conversation.

"What's up, Rob?" Carter answered.

"Got—information—need to know—important."

The static on the line cut into the conversation. "Hold on, Rob. You're cutting out." But the gist of Rob's conversation had been clear. Carter needed to get a better signal.

He pushed open the patio doors and stepped out onto the balcony. The signal bar went up one notch. "Can you hear me, Rob?"

"Yeah. That's better. Our conversation the other night kept nagging at me, so I called in a favor with a local cop I play poker with and had him check on the principals."

"I take it you didn't like what he found."

"No. Steven Adams, the father of the girl who accused Warren of molesting her, hasn't been to work for a week. His wife says he's in and out of the house, but she's sketchy on the times and dates that he's home."

"Is she covering for him?"

"My buddy says she looks scared, but it's hard to know if that's because she's covering or because she doesn't know what he's up to."

"Either way, that's not good."

"It gets worse. The father of the girl who was murdered after Warren was found not guilty, Larry Colbert, is a pharmaceutical sales rep. He was supposed to be at a convention in New Orleans for a week, but he never showed. His wife filed a missing-person report a couple of days ago."

Carter gripped the cell phone and tried to think. Two major players in the same tragedy—one missing and one with a sketchy alibi.

"Carter? You still there?"

"Yeah...just thinking."

"This looks really bad, man."

"I know."

"My buddy's name is Aaron Baker. I told him who you were and why I wanted the information. If you need anything, he said to tell you to call him directly. I'll text you his information."

"I appreciate it."

"Watch your back, Trahan. I want to collect on that drink you owe me."

"You got it."

He stepped back into the bedroom and secured the patio doors. As he turned around, Alaina walked into the room. She wore pink cotton shorts and a matching

T-shirt. Her damp hair trailed down her back and she wasn't wearing a stitch of makeup. Flip-flops separated her bare feet from the dirty floor, and it almost made him smile when he saw her toenails were painted the same color pink as her clothes.

Without a single bit of effort, Alaina LeBeau was the most attractive woman he'd ever known.

She was drying the end of her long tresses with a towel, but when she caught sight of him standing there, she froze. "What's wrong?" she asked.

He didn't want to scare her, but the time for hiding stuff was over. "I just got off the phone with an attorney friend of mine from Baton Rouge."

Her eyes flashed with anger. "You were checking up on me?"

"I suppose you can look at it that way, but I choose to think I was following up on anything that might follow you to Calais."

"You had no right!"

"I had every right. I have a responsibility to the citizens of Calais. If trouble followed you here, then it's my job to find it and eliminate the threat."

She glared at him for several seconds, but he'd seen the shift in her eyes. The anger was still there, but she knew he was right.

"Fine," she finally said. "Then I guess you already know about the Warren case."

"I found the particulars on the internet and asked my buddy about it from an attorney's perspective. After we talked, he contacted a friend of his with the Baton Rouge Police Department about the vandalism to your ex-boss's car."

He relayed the information he'd gotten from Rob.

The last remnant of anger dissolved from her expression and worry replaced it. "Both of them have disappeared? How can that be? What are the police doing?" Her voice rose as she talked.

He placed a hand on her arm. "The police are looking for them. They're taking this very seriously."

"Because of the case." She took a couple of steps forward and slumped down on the bed. "Sometimes I feel like my entire life is going to forever be defined by that one massive failure."

Carter studied her for a moment. He had plenty of bad things to say about defense attorneys. He couldn't even count the months he'd spent pursuing criminals only to have slick lawyers get them off on technicalities or bend lies so far it looked like the truth to gullible jurors. He'd assumed that Alaina was no different—that she'd done everything possible to win her case and it had come back to bite her in the rear. But after talking to Rob, and seeing how distressed she was now, he wondered just how wrong he'd gotten it.

He sat on the bed next to her. "The case wasn't your failure—it was your job."

"How can you say that? You were a cop in New Orleans— how many criminals you arrested got off because they had a good lawyer? Can you honestly tell me you felt no animosity toward me based on what I did for a living, even without knowing me at all?"

"It's true I wasn't happy when William told me your profession."

"See, even you—"

"But I was wrong," he interrupted her. "Not about all defense attorneys. I still think a lot would do anything this side of legal and some on the other side to win a case. But I don't think that about you. It's clear what happened eats at you. Is that why you quit?"

She shrugged. "Yes and no. My discontent with my job had been growing for a long time, but that case was like being hit in the face with a shovel. When Everett told me I was being passed over for the partnership I'd been promised, I knew exactly why and I knew no matter how much time passed, the partners would never forget."

Carter frowned. So far, Alaina's story matched up with Rob's suspicions about the fallout after the murder. "Did you ever wonder why you got assigned lead on that case?"

Alaina stared at him for a moment. "Not at the time. Everett had already told me I was up for the partnership when the old partner retired. I thought the case was a test—a way to make sure I was capable of handling anything that came my way."

"And what do you think now?"

A flash of anger passed over her face. "I think Everett made sure that no matter what happened, he wouldn't be responsible."

"I agree."

"You do?" She looked a bit surprised.

He nodded. "I'm sure you're good at your job, but it made no sense to put an attorney so green to criminal proceedings as the lead, especially on such a high-profile case."

She looked relieved and grateful and so vulnerable that his heart tugged. He ought to be disgusted. After all, her prowess in the courtroom had set a rapist free to claim one more victim, but it was impossible to remain angry when she was clearly distraught over what had happened.

"Was there any indication that the kid was insane?"

"No! There's a part of me that still can't wrap my mind around it. I spent hundreds of hours with him, talking about everything from his birth to the arrest for molesting that little girl. He was smart and funny. When the girl broke down on the stand, it only confirmed my belief that she was making up the story."

"Or lying about who the real perpetrator was."

Alaina nodded. "That crossed my mind more than once. But he had me fooled. He had me fooled but good."

"He had everyone fooled. The jury acquitted him."

"Based on the case I presented. I keep thinking, if I'd looked harder or if that girl hadn't broken down…"

"Did you push her to the breaking point?"

Alaina's eyes widened. "No! During break, Everett chewed me out for going too easy on her, but I told him I wouldn't be part of traumatizing the child more than she already was. I did believe she'd been molested. I just didn't think it was my client who did it."

"What happened after the break?"

"I don't know. Maybe it was just being in the same courtroom with her molester. She was only seven years old."

A tear slipped out of Alaina's eye and down her cheek. "She was barely older than I was when I was sent away from here to live with strangers. I was scared to death and I'd never been molested. How must that little girl have felt with everyone pushing her to relive the most frightening thing that had ever happened to her?"

Carter reached up and wiped the tear away with his finger. "You have to stop blaming yourself. You didn't know."

"But I should have." Her voice cracked and she began to cry.

Carter wrapped his arms around her and held her while she sobbed, stroking her hair with one hand. The dam had finally broken, and he knew she'd been holding it in all this time. It was far too much for one person to carry around with them. He knew that firsthand. In New Orleans, he'd been unable to escape the ghosts of all the people he couldn't save. Finally, he'd returned to Calais, attempting to outrun his past with distance.

It had taken a long time to adjust, but he was finally coming to peace with everything he'd seen.

"I'm sorry." Alaina pulled back a little and wiped her cheeks with her fingers, staring down at the floor. "I didn't mean to fall apart on you. Picking up the pieces of my disastrous life hardly falls under your favor to William."

Carter placed his hand under her chin and gently lifted her head until she looked at him. "Comforting you had nothing to do with William. And neither does this."

He lowered his lips to hers, softly kissing her.

Chapter Thirteen

Alaina stiffened slightly as Carter's lips brushed against hers. Then for the first time in her life, she allowed emotion to override logic and relaxed against him, pressing her body into his. He deepened the kiss, tasting her lips, then parting them with his own. She moaned as their tongues mingled together, then lifted her hand and ran her fingers through his hair.

He ran his fingers down her cheek and neck and then across her swollen breasts. She felt a rush of heat run through her center as his fingers brushed her hardened nipple. He moved his lips from hers and began to trail kisses down her neck, pursuing the path his fingers had followed just seconds before.

She reached for the bottom of her shirt and pulled it over her head. Even the thin cotton was too much fabric between them. He took a moment to look at her breasts and there was no doubt that he liked what he saw.

When he took her nipple in his mouth, shock waves ran through every square inch of her body and she gasped. "I want you," she whispered. "Now."

He rose from the bed and pulled off his clothes. The sight of his naked, toned body sent another wave of heat running through her, the anticipation making her almost dizzy. He pulled a condom from his wallet and rolled it on as she shrugged off her shorts and panties.

She lay back on the bed and he stood over her for a moment, taking in every square inch of her body. Then he moved over her and entered her in a single fluid motion. She cried out and dug her fingernails into his back as she felt the hard length of him press into her. Never had she wanted a man like this and never had a man made her feel so primal.

He lowered his lips to her again as he set the pace. She matched him in rhythm until they both tumbled over the edge.

CARTER MOVED to Alaina's side and stretched out beside her. He had never felt so sated—so satisfied—and from the look of pleasure on her face, he deduced Alaina felt the same. He wrapped his arm around her and pulled her close to him, tucking her body next to his.

"You were incredible," he whispered.

She smiled. "You're not so bad yourself. Who would have thought a defense attorney and a cop could have such chemistry?"

"Sometimes chemicals that don't mix properly lead to explosions. That was pretty explosive."

She laughed. "Maybe you're right. I've always played it safe with men in the past—stockbrokers, investment bankers—never anyone near the law enforcement arena. I didn't want my entire life to be about work."

He nodded. "I was the same way. Unfortunately, that presents problems, as well."

"Boy, does it. People who aren't in a related profession don't understand the intensity and the hours."

"And all the hours and intensity make it difficult to meet people outside of that arena."

"Exactly." She smiled. "Maybe we were both over-thinking it instead of making the obvious choice."

"Maybe, but before now, I still couldn't see myself with an attorney. Another cop, maybe."

"I suppose the answer is to keep the adversarial part of the relationship in the courtroom and not the bedroom."

He grinned. "There was nothing adversarial about what we just did, that's for sure."

He leaned over to kiss her. Despite the workout he'd just given her, she felt her body respond again.

"Round two?" he asked.

"I'm game if you are."

He ran his hand across her hips and pushed his body tighter into hers.

Then suddenly, his entire body tensed. She looked up at him, but as she opened her mouth to ask what was wrong, he laid a single finger across her lips. Immediately, her pulse spiked.

He slipped out of the bed and pulled on his jeans and shirt, then retrieved his pistol from the nightstand, where he'd left it earlier. "Stay here and lock the door behind me," he whispered before slipping silently out of the room.

Alaina hurried to the door as quickly as she could without noise. Carter had already disappeared downstairs in the darkness. She strained to make out any sound, but all she heard was the sound of her own heartbeat. But she knew Carter had heard something. He'd gone from erotic god to cop in a split second.

She eased the door shut and pulled the dead bolt into place. Then she shuffled back to the nightstand and took her own pistol from the drawer, checking the clip. She pulled on her shorts and T-shirt but didn't take the time to put on her tennis shoes. A quick scan of the room identified the far corner as the best tactical location. It offered a clear view of the bedroom and patio doors, and she could duck down behind the school desks.

Before sliding into her hiding place, she double-checked the patio doors. All was well, so she crouched behind the school desks, keeping a close watch on the bedroom door, her pistol clenched in her right hand.

She took in a deep breath and let it out slowly, trying to remain as calm as possible. Nervous people didn't shoot well. It felt like an eternity, but when she checked her watch, only minutes had passed. Her mind raced with all the possibilities of what could have drawn Carter's attention downstairs. None of the possibilities were good.

Why hadn't she insisted on going with him? If something happened, how was she supposed to even know unless it happened so loudly that she heard it upstairs and through the door? And while she had no doubt that Carter was skilled at his job, if someone knew how to get into and around the house without being seen, then they'd been working that angle for some time. No matter his skill set, Carter was still at a disadvantage.

Maybe she should go downstairs…in case he needed help. What was her other option? If something happened to Carter, she'd either have to get out alone or hide there, hoping the intruder didn't come after her. It would be a long night and even longer morning. Eventually, Carter's mother would send someone looking for them if he didn't appear the next morning, but that was far too much time for the intruder to strike.

Despite hours spent weekly at the gym, her thighs began to burn and she cursed her personal trainer for making her do all those clearly useless squats. Given the current situation, she'd have been better served taking a martial arts class or concentrating on sprinting.

Enough of hiding.

She'd been doing nothing but hiding her entire life—hiding from her past, hiding from her future, afraid to form meaningful relationships or permanent ties to any place. Her resignation from her position at the firm had as much to do with her unwillingness to commit to an unknown as it did anything else. Life was a constant risk. Sometimes you gambled and won, and sometimes you didn't.

Like tonight. She'd let her guard down with Carter and the time they'd shared had been incredible. Even though it couldn't work in the long run, she was glad she'd taken the chance and had that one special moment to remember. If she made it out of this house alive, she was going to start taking more chances—probably not the sexual kind—but risk was something she needed to get comfortable with.

She rose from her hiding place and crept over to the bedroom door. Pressing her ear against the thick wood, she strained to hear anything moving on the other side, but all was silent. She took a deep breath and blew it out, then slid the dead bolt back and eased the door open a crack. She peered outside but couldn't see beyond the edge of the stairwell, as that was as far as the hallway light extended.

Her hand tightened on her pistol and she slipped out the door and down the hall, hugging the wall as she shuffled. The creaking of the wood floors echoed throughout the house and her heart fell. The intruder would have no doubt where she was. The house would give her away. She paused for a moment to collect herself, then picked up the pace to the balcony, no longer concerned with hiding her movement.

She peered over the balcony and into the darkness below but couldn't make out anything but the dim shape of the furniture and art in the center of the entry. The downstairs lights had been on when she left the bathroom earlier. Had Carter turned them off to give himself cover or had the intruder planned another accident for her?

At the edge of the stairwell, she stooped down and ran her hand back and forth between the newels, ensuring that no wire was present. This time, the stairwell was free of wiring, but she knew the intruder may have constructed traps elsewhere in the house. Crouching next to the inside rail, she crept down the stairs until she reached the first floor.

As soon as her feet hit the marble floor, she scurried to a life-size suit of armor that stood against a nearby wall and huddled beside it. Her eyes were slowly adjusting to the dim light, turning the entry from black to hazy gray. Scanning the open area, she looked for any sign of movement, but everything was still.

Where was Carter?

She bit her lip, fighting the urge to call out his name. If he was on the trail of the intruder, her cries would ruin everything. Of course, her getting in the way could ruin everything, as well. She was beginning to think she should have stayed in the room. Her training was all about courtroom combat, not dark-spooky-house-gunfire combat.

Suddenly, a door hinge creaked throughout the tomb of silence and she jumped, covering her mouth with her free hand. Was it Carter or the intruder?

She scanned the open area, trying to determine where the noise had originated. It sounded as if it had come from the direction of the hallway leading to the laundry room, but the way sound echoed in the vast openness, she couldn't be sure. No matter, she couldn't stay where she was. The intruder's eyes would have already adjusted to the darkness, and he'd be able to easily spot where she was.

Her pulse racing, she slipped from behind the suit of

armor and crept down the wall, circling the downstairs. The first two doors to offshoot rooms were closed and she continued without pause, but the third door was open. Drawing up close to the edge of the opening, she held her breath, listening for any sound of movement inside.

One second, two seconds, three seconds.

She took a deep breath and hurried across the opening, but before she reached the other side, a hand clamped onto her shoulders. Her scream rang out in the open room, echoing back on her as loudly as it had left. She tried to spin and get a shot on him, but he grabbed her wrist, preventing her from raising her arm.

"It's me," Carter hissed into her ear.

She slumped against the wall and her breath came whooshing out. A wave of relief washed over her so strongly that it made her slightly dizzy. "Where is he?" she whispered.

"Get in this room and wait here."

She edged around the door opening and into the room as Carter slipped silently by. Her heart pounded so hard in her chest that it ached from the strain. Her hands shook and her breathing was still shallow. She had to get control.

Suddenly, the entry lights flicked on, flooding the downstairs with light. Carter stepped into the room seconds later and she felt the pounding in her chest lessen.

"Is he gone?" she asked.

"As far as I can tell."

"But he was inside the house, right? You heard him?"

He nodded. "I heard a tinkling sound, like glass breaking."

"Was it in the kitchen?"

"No, it was here." He pointed across the room to a window on the back wall. A single pane in the multipaned window was missing.

"He broke the pane to reach the lock on the window," she said.

"That's what he'd like us to think."

Alaina stared at the broken window. "What do you mean? That pane wasn't broken when I did my inspection, and you heard the glass breaking."

He nodded. "Yes, but he didn't get in the house through that window. It was broken from the inside. Look at the floor."

She scanned the floor below the window, but only a couple of flecks of glass reflected in the light. "But why?"

"To throw us off his real entry point. He didn't come through the doors—of that much I'm certain—and all the windows are still locked tight."

"There's another way into the house."

"Yeah. That's the only explanation."

Alaina's pulse spiked again and she slumped onto a chair next to the door, searching for another explanation—one that made her feel better about staying in this house for the rest of her time. "Maybe he was already inside the house when we got here this afternoon. Maybe he's been hiding all this time and just left."

"That crossed my mind, too, but I checked all the doors and windows. Nothing is unlocked, and there's no way he could have exited the house and locked the windows or doors behind him. Not without the keys or the ability to reach through glass."

"What about upstairs?" she asked, not wanting to let go of an answer that made her feel safer.

He shook his head. "He didn't have time to get back upstairs after breaking this window. I was out of the room too quickly and would have seen him."

"Unless he was using a secret passage, like the one from the laundry room to the master bedroom."

Carter frowned. "I suppose it's possible, but at the moment, I don't care. Let's get upstairs and grab whatever we need to leave. You're staying at my place tonight."

"I can't. I'll have to start over my two weeks and given how difficult they've been, I really want credit for the time I've already put in."

He glanced down at his watch. "It's past midnight. That's good enough for a day for me. We'll come back tomorrow morning. You could stay in town all day shopping and it counts, so why would it matter if part of the time you spend away is at night?"

"Well, I... Hmm." She couldn't think of a single logical argument against what Carter was saying.

"Besides," he continued, "no one even has to know. We can be back here before dawn."

"Then maybe we don't have to tell William?"

He nodded. "Or my mother."

Despite her anxiety, she smiled. "I wouldn't want to smear your reputation."

"I'm not sure it's good enough for a smearing to matter. Let's put on shoes at least, and I need to grab my keys."

"What about the window?"

"I don't have the tools to deal with it tonight and I'm sure Amos has been asleep for hours. Quite frankly, if someone wants to come in after we leave and roam all night, I don't care."

She blew out a breath. "Then let's get going."

CARTER PUSHED OPEN the door to his cabin and stepped back, allowing Alaina to enter. It was close to 1:00 a.m. and they were both beyond exhausted. She hesitated a millisecond, then stepped into his living room and waited as he closed the door and locked it. He'd left a lamp on in the living room, but one look at her stiff posture and he knew the dim light only reminded her of what they'd fled from.

He flipped on the ceiling fan lights and the room lit up. Her shoulders relaxed a bit and he pointed to two doors on the right side of the room. "The first door's the bathroom. Second is the bedroom. Kitchen ahead of you and that's pretty much it."

She scanned the tiny cabin but he could tell by the way she picked at a loose thread on the bottom of her T-shirt that her mind was miles away.

"Do you want something to drink?"

"No," she said, her voice quiet and emotionless.

He stepped over to her and put his hands on her shoulders. "This is going to be all right."

She shook her head. "You can't know that. What if it's finally time for me to pay the piper?"

"You know what's happening is not right. There is no great karmic reckoning. Whoever is stalking you is breaking the law and he's going to pay for that. I'm going to make sure of it."

She nodded but didn't look convinced. "I'm really tired. Can we just go to bed?"

"Sure." He took her hand and led her into the bedroom. "You're in luck. I washed all the linens yesterday."

He waited for a smile, even a small one, but she just stood there clutching her purse. "Go ahead and get comfortable. I'm going to make a quick check of everything and get a drink. I'll be back in a couple of minutes."

She placed her purse on the dresser and kicked off her sandals, then slipped under the covers. He reached for the bedroom light, but she sat up and shook her head. "Leave it on, please."

"Sure." He left the light on and headed for the kitchen. The cold beer was tempting but not a good idea. Given the disadvantage he'd have, Carter didn't think the intruder would come looking for Alaina at his cabin, but he couldn't be sure. It wasn't worth the risk to dull his senses, even by only one beer.

He grabbed a bottled water instead and took a gulp, letting the cold liquid run down his dry throat. Staring out his kitchen window into the swamp, he ran through the night. So many things had happened in such a short span of time—so many lines crossed that should never have been crossed.

If he said he regretted sleeping with Alaina, he'd be lying. Their passion had been incredible—more intense and pleasurable than he'd ever experienced before. He'd never regret that, but he did feel guilty.

Alaina was scared and anxious, with her entire life at a crossroads. He worried that in a saner state she wouldn't have made the choice she made tonight. Clearly, she was in shock now and he imagined most of it was because of the intruder. But what if some of that shock was attributed to having sex with him?

He'd added another layer for an already-overloaded mind to deal with, and for that, he felt bad. From this point on, he'd be the professional he was supposed to be. When this was all over and Alaina was safe, he'd let her decide if she wanted to revisit what had happened between them tonight.

He turned from the kitchen window and caught sight of his laptop on the kitchen table. His body wanted to join Alaina in bed, but his mind was whirling so hard on overload that he knew sleep wouldn't come quickly or well. He walked over to the bedroom and peeked inside. Alaina was curled up on her side, her breathing deep. Exhaustion and stress had finally gone into overdrive and her body had shut down to recuperate. He'd been there many times before.

Likely, she'd sleep through until morning, which meant if he wanted to take the time to do some research on the two missing suspects, he had the bandwidth. If she awakened, he'd be close enough at the kitchen table to hear her. He reached for the lamp on the dresser and clicked it on, then turned off the overhead light. She never stirred.

Satisfied that she was safe and resting, he headed into the kitchen and opened his laptop. Somewhere, there had to be a clue. All day it had nagged at him that he was missing something. It was there, just under the surface. He just had to expose it.

The sooner this was over, the sooner he could address his feelings for Alaina. He wasn't even going to lie to himself that it was just a physical attraction. That was definitely part of it, but it went deeper than that.

When this was over, he'd figure out just how deep.

Chapter Fourteen

Alaina ran down the stairwell in the dark. The boom of thunder sounded all around her and her head felt as if it would burst with each blast. It seemed she'd been running down the stairs forever, trying to escape something that pursued her. Something she couldn't see.

The first floor was hidden from her, lost in a haze of gray, but she knew it was there. If only she could run faster...harder...she'd make it off the stairs. She strained to see the marble floor in the darkness, certain it was only inches away.

"You look for the wrong things."

Her mother's voice caused her to slow.

"I look for peace and happiness," she replied.

"You cannot have peace and happiness without truth."

"But what is the truth?"

"It's there. It's always been there."

She stopped running and strained to hear her mother's voice as it began to fade away. "Wait, don't go!"

"The truth is inside of you...inside of you...inside of you..."

The voice echoed in her head, then faded away to silence.

ALAINA BOLTED UPRIGHT in the bed, her heart pounding in her chest. A second wave of panic washed over her when she realized she didn't recognize anything about her surroundings. She flung back the covers and jumped out of bed, then remembered she was at Carter's house... in Carter's bed.

Last night!

It all came back to her in a flash—the intruder, their flight from the house.

Having sex with Carter.

What in the world had she been thinking? The last thing she needed to do was complicate her life any more. Everything was a muddled mess—lacking so much clarity that now even her dreams were muddled.

The truth is inside of you.

Yeah, right. If she'd been carrying around the answer to her seriously screwed life, wouldn't she have found it by now? Instead, she'd quit a perfectly good, if limited, job and relocated to the middle of a swamp where she was being harassed by a mystery intruder and protected by a cop who had a natural distrust and dislike for attorneys, but whom she'd had earth-shattering sex with the night before.

Oh, the truth was definitely inside of her. She was an idiot.

She flipped the covers back over the bed. From the looks of things, she'd spent the rest of the night alone. The other side of the bed showed no signs of recent occupancy. Vaguely, she remembered Carter stating he'd join her shortly, but he must be on man time. Like when men said they'd call you tomorrow and the call came two weeks later.

Frustrated at the level of chaos that was now her life, she headed into the living room to see if Carter was anywhere in sight and if he kept coffee in his bachelor pad. It took only one step out of the bedroom to spot him slumped over the kitchen table, arms crossed under his head, and dead asleep. A little of her aggravation wore off at the sight of the open laptop in front of him. He'd probably spent hours combing the internet for information that might help them and had fallen asleep sitting there.

Whatever faults Carter may have, apparently lack of dedication to his job wasn't one of them. She eased across the living room to the kitchen, not wanting to startle him, but as she stepped into the breakfast nook, the hardwood floors creaked beneath her.

Carter jumped up from the table, grabbing his pistol with one hand and her arm with the other. Surprised at the speed and intensity of his movement, she gasped. In a split second, he released her arm.

"I'm sorry," he said as he placed the pistol back on the table.

"Occupational hazard?"

"Yeah, I guess so." He ran one hand through his hair. "I didn't realize I fell asleep."

"I was trying to wake you without startling you, but I wasn't exactly successful."

"No, it's my fault. I should have called it quits and gone to bed a long time ago." He stretched his arms above his head and tilted his head from side to side. "I'll probably have a stiff neck the rest of the day."

Dark circles were beginning to form under his eyes and his face showed the strain he felt. A wave of guilt washed over her. She'd blown into this man's life and upset the balance to the point that the life he'd previously enjoyed had now become a strain.

"I'm sorry my personal problems are interfering so much with your normal life. I never thought when I came here that things would get so weird."

"It's not your fault."

"Isn't it? Whatever is going on is because of me—whether I brought it with me or my presence prompted someone who was already here to go off the rails—either way, it's still my coming to Calais that set the wheels in motion."

"That still doesn't place the blame on you. Whatever is going on is only the fault of the perpetrator. I'm surprised to hear an attorney, of all people, putting forth a blame-the-victim argument."

She sighed. Nothing was worse than when someone threw your profession back in your face and was right about it. "I'm not arguing. I just figured you probably left New Orleans to get away from this sort of aggravation and I've brought it right to your front door—or into your kitchen—however you want to look at it."

He looked down at the floor for a moment, then back up at her. "I suppose it sounds bad if I say that I'm kind of enjoying the change of pace, right?"

He looked so guilty that she had to smile. "So the small-town thing *does* get dull."

"That doesn't mean I'm happy that someone's harassing you," he hurried to explain. "You could have been killed the other night."

She sobered a bit. "I know you're not happy about it, but all the same, I'm really glad you're the one here handling it. Your experience is a big advantage and one that most perpetrators wouldn't expect in such a small place."

"Doesn't seem like much of an advantage at the moment."

"Well, it is, and that's my professional opinion. No arguing."

He gave her a small smile. "I wouldn't dream of arguing with an attorney."

"Good, then please tell me you have something to eat

in here. I really don't feel like returning to that mauso-
leum on an empty stomach."

"Uh-oh."

"Don't tell me this is really and truly a bachelor's pad."
She walked over to the refrigerator and opened it. "Beer
and pizza. You're living a cliché, Trahan."

"If you're going to live a cliché, that's a good one."

She smiled. "You have a point, but what you do not
have is eggs, a bagel or even a loaf of bread."

He nodded. "My mom keeps telling me that if I got
married, I could count on eating on a regular basis."

She raised an eyebrow. "Or two people could count
on starving."

He grinned. "It's just one of her many lines. She knows
better than to assume anyone wants to cook. For her, it's
an art form, but for others, it's just another chore. I usually eat breakfast at the café, but if you're not comfortable with that…"

She frowned. "I ate there yesterday. Surely, you don't
think Jack is going to make a scene at his workplace?"

"No. I was thinking more about our showing up there
at dawn, in the same vehicle…"

"Oh!" She felt a tiny blush run up her neck. "Well,
Connie's more likely to give me a high five than a disap-
proving look, and Jack doesn't like me anyway."

He stepped closer to her and ran one finger down her
arm. "And it's not like any supposition about last night
would be incorrect."

Her skin tingled at the light touch of his finger and she
felt her knees weaken, along with her resolve to avoid a
repeat of last night. Suddenly aware of the small amount
of thin fabric that separated her more sensitive parts from
his hand, she inched back just a bit.

She didn't mean to insult him, but from the way he

dropped his hand and stepped away from her, she was certain that was exactly what she'd done. Holding in a sigh, she stepped around him and headed for the bedroom.

"Let me put on my shoes," she said.

Carter's reaction was exactly why they had no business playing games. Too much was at stake to play things fast and loose. It might seem like fun now, but what would that bit of fun cost them in the long run? Maybe Carter could view it as a pleasurable fling. At one time, she would have been able to, as well. But something about the sexy sheriff made her want more and that wasn't something she was in a position to pursue right now. Everything about her life was in flux. The last thing she needed to do was drag someone into her mess.

When she exited the bedroom, Carter was standing in the living room holding his truck keys. "We'll grab some breakfast, then go back to the house. I want to take a look around, but I have other responsibilities, so I can't be there all day. If you're not comfortable, you're welcome to stay with my mother."

"I'm sure I'll be fine. It appears he prefers the cover of night for his monkey business."

Carter nodded and opened the front door to allow her out. He was silent the entire ride to the café, and Alaina couldn't help but wonder what was running through his mind. He stared out the windshield directly ahead of them, almost scowling at the road. Either he was aggravated with the situation, with her or with both. She was betting on both.

Connie raised her eyebrows when they walked in the café together and took seats at the counter. "So, late night?" she asked as she poured coffee and slid it in front of them.

Alaina took a sip of the black coffee without even adding sweetener, then sighed. "You have no idea."

Something in Alaina's tone must have conveyed anything but a night of carnal pleasure. Connie's expression went from sly approval to immediate concern. "Is everything all right?" she asked.

Alaina looked over at Carter, wondering if she was supposed to keep the information quiet. It was something she should have thought to ask on the way over, but with his acting so weird, it hadn't occurred to her that they might need to get their stories straight beforehand.

Carter stared at the wall behind the counter, not even aware of their conversation.

"Carter?" She poked him with her elbow and he blinked.

"Sorry. Lost in thought."

"Connie wants to know if everything is all right," she said, hoping he understood the question buried in her statement.

"I see." He shrugged. "No use in hiding it. Things tend to get around Calais whether you want them to or not."

"Okay," Connie said, clearly worried, "will someone please tell me what's going on?"

"I've apparently got an unwelcoming committee at the house," Alaina said and told Connie some of the things that had transpired over the past few days—careful to leave out the part about her romp with Carter the night before.

"So Carter stayed there last night to protect you?" Connie asked.

"Yes," Alaina said and left it at that. If people knew she hadn't stayed at the estate the night before, someone who felt they'd been screwed by her stepfather may try to make an issue of it.

"Wow," Connie said. "That's really awful. I mean, I know people around here didn't like your stepfather—I've been here long enough to hear the stories—but he cut you out of what was yours for a long time. I don't get why anyone would have a problem with you."

"It's more likely that trouble followed me here."

Connie's eyes widened. "Oh! You mean something to do with when you were an attorney?"

"It's possible."

"You're not going back there, are you?"

"I don't have a choice. If I quit now, I'll have to start this all over again later on and if the problem is something I brought with me, it will just follow me somewhere else. I may as well deal with it now."

Connie nodded and glanced at the clock on the wall. "Well, let me cook you two some breakfast. I don't know when Jack will show up and the regulars won't be in for another twenty minutes or so."

"If it's no trouble," Alaina said, "that would be great."

She glanced over at Carter, who still stared straight ahead at the wall behind the grill. His silence bothered her. Either he was angry over her unintentional brush-off this morning or he was more worried about the situation than he was letting on. Neither were good options.

They sat in silence as Connie cooked up two specials and placed them in front of them. The waitress glanced over at Carter, then back at Alaina and raised her eyebrows. Alaina shrugged. She had no idea what had gotten into the brooding sheriff and didn't want to guess.

"I need to get some stock from the back," Connie said. "Are you two all right for a couple of minutes?"

"We're fine," Alaina said. "Thanks."

Connie hurried off to the storeroom at the back of the restaurant, and Alaina began to eat her breakfast in silence. She'd finished a little over half of it when the ringer sounded on her phone.

A phone call! Service must be available again.

She pulled the phone out of her purse and checked the display. Five missed calls, one phone message and a text sent only minutes ago. Her pulse quickened as she clicked on the text message. A text this early in the morning could only mean something bad.

Call me as soon as you can. Everett.

"Is everything all right?" Carter's voice broke into her thoughts.

"It's a text from Everett. He wants me to call him."

Carter frowned. "A text this early?"

"Yeah. There are some missed calls from yesterday. I bet everything's coming through at one time."

She located Everett's number in the contact list and pressed Call. Maybe it was good news. Maybe they'd caught the vandal and he was calling to let her know the worry was over. But as soon as she heard his voice, she knew something was wrong.

"Alaina, thank God! I was about to call that sheriff you told me about."

She clenched the cell phone. "What's wrong?"

"Emily Jensen was attacked in the parking lot of her apartment building last night."

"No!" The kind intern wouldn't even kill bugs when they got in the office. The last thing she should be on the receiving end of was violence. "Is she all right?"

"She's in a coma."

Alaina's heart dropped and she choked back a sob.

"It's touch and go," Everett said, "but for now, she's stable."

"Did they catch her attacker?"

"No, and there were no cameras at her apartment building."

"Have the police made any progress at all?"

Everett sighed. "I'm afraid not. The two main suspects are Steven Adams and Larry Colbert, who are both apparently lost in the wind. I sent my wife and daughter to her mother's in Phoenix and stepped up security around the building. If I'd thought for a minute that they'd go after Emily..."

"You couldn't have known. It makes no sense to take it out on her."

"No, it doesn't. Well, I've got to get ready for a trial this morning, and I haven't slept at all. Emily is at Park Memorial Hospital if you want to send a card. I'll call you as soon as I have an update on anything."

"Thanks. And, Everett, watch your back."

"Yeah."

Carter had been staring at her during the entire conversation, knowing the news wasn't good. "What happened?" he asked.

Alaina told him about Emily, choking back a sob when she got to the part about the girl being in a coma.

"Did Emily work on the Warren case?"

"No. I mean, indirectly, Emily works on every case. She's an intern, so she does all the document cataloging, but she's rarely in court except when she requests to watch the proceedings, and she certainly wasn't in court for that case."

"Really? I would think an aspiring attorney would want to be on the ground floor of a criminal case."

"Emily has no interest in pursuing criminal law. She intends to enter the nonprofit sector. She just hasn't exactly told Everett that. They would never waste their time and education on helping others, but for Emily, the internship at such a prestigious firm will open practically any door she wants."

"Sounds like you were close. I'm really sorry."

Alaina swallowed, the lump in her throat making it ache. "I was closer to her than the others, but that's not saying a lot. She's a very private person and I'm a very guarded person, but I like and respect her. She's so nice."

Her voice broke and she choked back a sob. "She doesn't deserve this!"

Carter placed his hand on hers. "Of course she doesn't."

"I have to go see her."

Carter shook his head. "That's not a good idea. He may have attacked Emily hoping to draw you out."

"If he doesn't know where I am, then who's harassing me here?"

"I don't know, and I don't like all these moving pieces. But if I were stalking you, the one place I'd be watching is that hospital."

She blew out a breath, trying to control her frustration. He was right, but that didn't mean she had to like it.

"Were the missed calls from Everett? You told him to call the sheriff's department if he couldn't reach you, right?"

"Yeah. I don't know why he didn't call for me there."

She scrolled through the missed calls, and her pulse quickened when she saw the first one was from Emily. "Emily called me yesterday evening from the law office."

"Did she leave a message?"

"No."

"Turn off your phone and turn it back on. Just to make sure there's nothing hanging out there in cell limbo."

She powered down the phone, waited ten seconds, then powered it back up, eyes glued to the message window at the bottom. When the message indicator popped up, she jumped on her seat. "There's a message!"

"Stay calm," Carter directed. "It may be from Everett."

Some of the wind left her sails. "You're right," she said as she punched the button to check the message. Emily's voice sounded through the phone a second later.

Alaina, I'm really sorry to call you like this, but I need to talk to you. I found something I don't understand...it doesn't look good, but maybe I'm misunderstanding what I'm seeing. I know you will be able to make sense of it. You're the smartest person I know. And this involves you. Please call me as soon as you get this message.

Alaina's heart dropped as Emily's message played. What in the world had the intern stumbled into? She hit Replay and handed the phone to Carter. He listened to the message, his expression becoming graver as the seconds passed.

"I don't like it," he said as he handed the cell phone back to her. "Do you know what cases Emily was working on when you left?"

"It could have been anything. A first-year intern is nothing more than a glorified administrative assistant really. Emily did a lot of filing and labeling and assembling documents for court, but she wasn't involved in the analysis of any of them."

"But she may have reviewed them if she had the time."

"Certainly. The way most interns learn is by seeing how the lead attorney has developed the case." She took a breath and tensed her back, ready to argue. "You realize this means I have to go see her now."

"She's in a coma."

"At this moment, but she may wake up."

Carter frowned, but she could see the wheels turning. "If she wanted to talk to you about a case, she probably had the case documents with her. I could talk to the officer assigned to the case and see if I can get a copy of the documents recovered at the scene."

"That would be great!"

"Don't get excited just yet. They don't have to give me anything, but I'm hoping if I explain the situation here and ask nicely that they will."

"We have to try."

Carter nodded and pulled some money from his wallet. "Let's head to the house. I'll do a cursory check while you change clothes, but anything more intense will have to wait until we get back. I don't have anyone who has the training or authority to do it for me."

"I wouldn't want anyone else in there anyway. It may be dangerous for them."

"I agree. We'll inform Amos of the situation on the way out—tell him to take a day off."

Connie came out of the storeroom as Alaina was pulling her purse over her shoulder. "Was my cooking that bad? Neither of you finished your breakfast."

"I have an emergency back in Baton Rouge, but the breakfast was great."

Carter nodded. "You keep cooking and Jack might be out of a job."

"Thanks," Connie told Carter, "but I'm not interested in doing more work, so my cooking will be our secret. I hope things turn out all right in Baton Rouge."

"Me, too," Alaina said.

But she was already worried. What had Emily seen that caused her so much distress? And did it have anything to do with the attack on her?

She hoped answers lay in Baton Rouge because all she'd found in Calais were questions.

Chapter Fifteen

Carter hurried down the hospital stairs to a coffee shop on the first floor, leaving Alaina in Emily's room, waiting on the doctor to make his rounds. The lead detective on the case had agreed to meet him there, wanting to speak to Alaina as well in case she could provide any information about the attack on Emily. Carter had explained that they were there to get information and likely had nothing to give, but the detective wanted to talk to them anyway.

Carter understood the direction he was taking. Often, people had no idea how much information they possessed because they only had one or two pieces of a large puzzle. But the detective was collecting all the pieces he could and hopefully would form a picture that led to an arrest. Detective work was rarely as portrayed in the movies or books. Mostly, it was tedious and arrests were made over the details and not great leaps of intuition.

The detective wore street clothes, as was often the case when they were canvassing for information, but Carter picked him out of the coffee shop crowd in a matter of seconds. Something about the way cops studied everything while appearing not to and the way they positioned themselves for optimum defense regardless of the situation—it was almost like breathing. He wasn't sure they could hide it if they wanted to.

As he crossed the shop, the detective spotted him as well and nodded, then pointed to a table in the corner. Carter stopped at the counter to grab a coffee and headed over to join the detective, who was already working on a big cup himself.

"Carter Trahan," Carter said as he took his seat and extended his hand across the table.

"John Breaux," the detective said as he gave Carter's hand a shake. "I appreciate your meeting me."

"I don't know if I can help, but you are welcome to anything I have."

"How is Ms. Jensen?"

"She's still unconscious but her vitals are stable. The doctors think she will awaken. They just have no idea when."

"That's good news compared to last night."

"I noticed you had a guard at her room. Are you planning to keep one there?"

"Until someone is arrested, absolutely. Given Ms. Jensen's connections with the law firm and the threat on Mr. Winstrom, we can't assume this was a random attack. Unconscious in that bed, she's a sitting duck."

"I'm glad she'll have protection. Alaina wanted me to make sure that was the case. If you get short-staffed or get the order from above to pull the security detail, let me know. Alaina said she'd pay for private security herself."

"I hope it doesn't come to that, but I appreciate Ms. LeBeau's offer and will definitely let you know if the situation changes. You said Ms. LeBeau has had some problems since her arrival in Calais?"

Carter nodded and gave John a rundown of the things that had transpired since Alaina's residency at the estate.

"Is it possible someone local is responsible?" John asked when Carter finished.

"Sure, and I have someone in mind whom I'm keeping an eye on. He was expecting to inherit but Alaina's step-father didn't have the right to distribute the estate. It was all set in stone by her mother, who was the heir."

"Will he inherit if the sisters don't meet their obliga-tions?"

"Not that I'm aware of and he wouldn't be either, as the terms of the will have been kept confidential. But the person I'm talking about isn't all that stable. He's childish, at best, and at worst, a professional alcoholic."

"So he might do it just for sport—if he can't have it, then they won't either."

Carter nodded. "That's what I was thinking."

"Makes sense, but I still want to cover all bases."

"I would, too. What can you tell me about the attack?"

"Ms. Jensen left work at 6:00 p.m. and went to her gym. She worked out for approximately an hour, then had smoothies with some acquaintances for another hour. It was just getting dark when she parked at her apartment."

"No security cameras, right?"

"No. It's a decent building but old. It doesn't have the amenities of newer developments, but it's near the college and the rent's cheap, so it tends to be filled up mostly by college students."

"No one saw anything?"

"I'm headed back over there after this to finish can-vassing. Between classes and their social lives, it's hard to pin down an entire building of students. But so far, no one who was in the building at the time of the attack saw or heard a thing except the girl who called the police."

"And what did she see?"

"She has an apartment on the side facing the parking lot where the attack occurred. She was on her balcony watering a plant. The lighting in the lot is not substantial, so she didn't see the strike, but when she heard Ms. Jensen scream, she scanned the lot and saw someone clad in jeans and a black hooded sweatshirt running across the lot and away from the building. Then she saw Ms. Jensen collapsed next to her car and she called 9-1-1."

Carter shook his head. "A building of college students doesn't seem like a good mark for a thief. Did you find any prints?"

"No. It may be that he didn't touch anything we could print, or it may be that he was wearing gloves. The witness couldn't be sure on that point."

"Her purse was taken?"

"The receptionist at the law office said Ms. Jensen carried a purse and sometimes a briefcase. There was no sign of either at the law office, the gym or her apartment, so I'm assuming both were taken."

John frowned.

"What?" Carter asked. "You have that look like something doesn't sit right with you."

"Yeah. It could be nothing, but Ms. Jensen was wearing a diamond necklace. It was her mother's and the stone was a pretty good size. I figure if it was a random theft, he would have pulled it off her neck. The chain was thin."

"Maybe she screamed and he bolted before he could steal the necklace."

"Maybe, but the situation doesn't fit tweaker or professional."

Carter nodded. "Which leads to the attack being personal and not made by a professional."

"Yeah, but then why steal her bags? If the same person who threatened Mr. Winstrom is responsible for attacking Ms. Jensen, why make it look like a robbery in one case when he bragged about his work in another?"

"I have no idea, but I don't like it."

John blew out a breath and leaned back in his chair. "I don't either. I'm glad to hear another law enforcement professional say that, because the chief thinks I'm out on a limb here. But I can feel it—something isn't right about this case."

"I'm at the same place with the situation in Calais. On the surface, it looks like a fairly simple case of jealousy, but I feel like I'm missing something."

John nodded. "Like something's moving just below the surface."

"Exactly."

"Do you think our cases are related?" John asked.

"I don't know, but I intend to find out."

ALAINA DOWNED the last of her iced cappuccino and set the glass back on the coffee shop table with a sigh. Detective Breaux had left just a minute before, no closer to knowing what was going on than he had been before speaking with her.

"I wish I could do something," she said. "I kept saying 'I don't know' over and over to all Detective Breaux's questions. I feel so useless."

"Every little bit helps," Carter said.

"Helps what? Add more useless information for him to sift through?"

"You sift through tons of data all the time putting a case together. You know firsthand that what seems irrelevant to the layperson could be the item that brings you a conviction."

"Perhaps, but when I'm sifting, the crime has already been committed. I'm not up against a time clock trying to prevent it from happening again."

"We all have our roles to play. It doesn't do you any good to put yourself down. You're doing what you can."

"Am I? Because I can't stop thinking if I'd only gone into town to check my messages yesterday, or if I'd gotten to know Emily better so I could guess at what she wanted, or if I'd never made the impulsive decision to quit my job and move to the swamp in the first place—"

"Maybe she wouldn't have been attacked?" Carter finished.

"Maybe." She blew out a breath. "I know it sounds ridiculous when you say it out loud, but I can't help how I feel."

"No, but I'm still going to tell you that you're wrong."

She gave him a small smile, knowing he was trying to make her feel better. "So what now?"

Carter stared out the window and frowned. She turned and saw a woman walk in front of them on the sidewalk carrying a briefcase.

"Why did she carry a briefcase?" Carter asked. "Wouldn't a backpack be more normal fare for a college student, even one in law?"

Alaina nodded. "I had a pink one with bright yellow flowers."

Carter smiled. "I can see that."

"Emily had the briefcase for her work at the firm. I don't think she used it for school. She usually left it at the office unless she was taking something home with her."

"Like last night?"

"If the receptionist saw her with it, then I guess so."

"Is there any way to tell what she was working on?"

Alaina frowned. "I suppose I could ask Everett, but why?"

"Just thinking. With a random robbery, the perp usually removes anything of value and ditches the containers, but the police didn't find either in the vicinity."

"Maybe he jumped in a car and left. Anyway, I don't see how it would help to find them unless he left a print."

"No, but I was thinking about the message Emily left for you. She said she'd found something that didn't look good. Given that she called you right after she left the office, we can assume it's something she saw at work."

Alaina straightened in her chair. "And you think she brought whatever it was with her?"

"It would make sense. If her attack is related to information contained in those documents, it would help to know what documents she'd taken with her."

A wave of frustration coursed through her. "But Everett wouldn't know what she had, especially if she was bringing it for me to see."

She looked across the street and her pulse quickened. "I have an idea."

"Why does that look on your face make me think I'm not going to like it?"

"If you don't, you can sit here and pretend I never told you." She nodded her head toward the window. "Across the street is an internet café. They have a couple of computers available for anyone to use. I could log in to the law firm's server remotely and see what Emily copied before she left for the day. She would never have risked removing originals from the firm."

"How can you see the copies?"

"As a safety feature, the copier automatically creates a scanned backup of anything processed, either by copying or documents sent to print from a PC."

Carter's expression cleared in understanding. "So you could see everything she copied that day."

"Exactly."

He frowned. "But surely they deleted your network passwords after you resigned."

"I'm sure they did, but one of the attorneys there has coffee at that internet café all the time because he's chasing a doctor who works at this hospital. He just left that café."

"So? I still don't get how that helps."

"He's an idiot. I can probably guess his password and if anyone checks the server logs, they'll think it was him. Everyone at the firm knows about the doctor and the café."

"So you want to hack into your old employer's server—the most prestigious law firm in Baton Rouge—using a coworker's credentials."

She bit her lower lip. "Yes."

He smiled. "I like it. And I promise I didn't see a thing."

She grabbed her purse and they hurried across the street to the café. Although they were already coffee-logged, Carter bought two cups so that nothing appeared out of place. Alaina snagged a computer in a remote corner of the café and went to work. It took only a minute for her to figure out Kurt's password and gain access to the system.

Carter's eyes widened when the law firm logo appeared at the top of the page. "Wow, you weren't lying. What's his password—123456?"

She rolled her eyes. "Hotguy."

Carter stared. "You're kidding me."

"If only I were. This is the idiot who got the promotion that should have been mine."

"That's just wrong, but his incompetence may come in handy now."

She clicked through the printer queue, scanning for Emily's passcode. "Here's Emily's code." She pointed to a numbered link, then clicked on it.

As she scanned the documents, her spirit began to flag.

They were all blank forms for packets they gave to new clients. Maybe her theory was wrong.

When she got to the last entry in the log, she sucked in a breath.

"What is it?" Carter asked.

"The Warren case. She copied all the interviews with the defendant, his parents and the parents of the victim."

He shook his head. "And we come full circle—right back to the Warren case. Maybe the attack on Emily *was* related to the vandalism of Everett's car. If one of those victims' fathers is mentally off—and it's a good possibility in either case—they wouldn't necessarily make rational decisions."

"And Emily is the easiest target because she's the only one who doesn't live somewhere with security and guards." She blew out a breath. "Damn it! I thought we were onto something."

He placed on hand on her shoulder. "We are onto something. Every little bit helps and this answers at least one question in your mind. Now you know what Emily wanted to speak to you about."

"No…I mean, I still don't. I have no idea what Emily saw in those files that bothered her and I've been over them a hundred times."

"Maybe it was something she didn't understand because she hasn't been at it long enough. Likely, it was something you could have easily explained."

"So the attack on her had nothing to do with me?"

"We have no way of knowing for certain, but taking this into account, it doesn't look that way."

"So what do we do now?"

"You check on Emily one last time and then we figure out what to do about that security risk you're living in."

"What about Detective Breaux? Should we tell him what we found?"

"I don't think computer hacking is something we should admit to a detective, even one who's on our side. But I will tell him what you told me about the scanned backup. He can check with the firm and legally acquire the information."

"Sounds like a plan."

They rose from their chairs and walked back across the street to the hospital, where they made their way to the third floor. Alaina waved at the trauma nurse who was on duty at the desk and they turned down the hallway to the right to go to Emily's room.

Carter froze for a moment, then hurried down the hall, pointing at the empty guard's chair in front of Emily's door. Alaina's pulse quickened and she stepped up her pace to a jog to keep up with his long strides.

Just as they reached Emily's room, the monitors attached to Emily set off their alarms. Alaina burst into the hospital room right in front of Carter and drew up short at the sight of Kurt McGraw standing right next to Emily's bed.

Chapter Sixteen

"What the hell are you doing?" Alaina yelled as she raced over to the hospital bed.

Kurt's eyes widened and he took a step back from the bed. "Nothing, I swear. I hadn't even said a word and then everything went off."

The trauma nurse rushed into the room and ordered them all out. A harried doctor pushed past them as they exited the room and gathered in the hallway.

"Where is the guard?" Carter demanded.

Kurt put his hands up in a defensive manner, clearly cluing in on Carter's anger. "There was no one here when I came up. I swear."

A groan sounded in the room behind them and they looked over as the guard stumbled against the doorway, clutching his head with his hands.

"What happened?" Carter asked.

The guard slumped back down in his chair. "There was a doctor. He asked me to help him move something in this room, but when I got in here, he clocked me with something heavy."

"A doctor?" Alaina stared at the guard. "Why in the world would a doctor do something like that?"

Carter's expression was grim. "They wouldn't, but if someone wanted an opportunity to get at Emily, all they had to do was snag a set of scrubs from the lockers and say they were a doctor." He looked up at Kurt.

"I swear, it wasn't me!" Kurt said. "I don't even know that man."

"But you knew he was guarding Emily. With him out of the way, you had a clear shot at her."

Kurt paled, his mind finally wrapping around the enormity of Carter's implication. "You've got it all wrong. I came to the hospital to see someone I'm dating. I thought I'd check on Emily before I left. There was no guard in that chair."

"Uh-huh." Carter tapped the guard on the shoulder. "Does this man look like the doctor who clocked you?"

The guard looked up at Kurt and squinted, then sighed. "I don't remember. My memory's all hazy. Maybe?"

Alaina shook her head. "That won't do us any good."

"Jeez, Alaina!" Kurt stared at her. "You can't possibly think I did this. I like Emily. Why would I want to hurt her?"

"Someone did. They hurt her last night and came back today to finish the job."

Before Kurt could reply, the trauma nurse came out of Emily's room.

"How is she?" Alaina asked.

"We've gotten her stabilized, but she was injected with something that affected her heart. We won't know more until we finish running tests." Her expression hardened. "In the meantime, I need all of you to exit this floor. We're restricting access to medical personnel only."

"There may be a problem with that," Carter said and explained what had happened to the guard.

The nurse's eyes widened. "I'll call hospital security and have them check the video and lock all the stairwells on the inside. If anyone wants to get down these halls, they'll have to get past me."

Carter nodded. "I'm going to call Detective Breaux. He's in charge of Emily's case and he'll need to get another guard out here—two, if I can talk him into it."

"I appreciate that," she said, "but I'm still going to need you all to leave. The more people milling around, the more chance someone can slip through."

They all trailed down the hall to the elevator and went down to the first floor. As they stepped into the lobby, Detective Breaux rushed through the door.

"What happened?"

Carter gave him a rundown of the events. Detective Breaux listened intently and gave Kurt a long once-over when the story turned to his part. When Carter finished, Detective Breaux looked at Kurt.

"I'll start with you," the detective said. "We can talk in the cafeteria." He looked at Carter. "And I'll call for another guard. The captain can't argue the necessity after this."

"Do you need anything else from us?" Carter asked.

"Not at the moment. Will you be in town much longer?"

"We weren't planning on it," Carter replied.

Detective Breaux nodded. "If you need to get back home, that's fine. I can take your statements over the phone and have you sign them later."

Kurt, who'd grown more frustrated under the scrutiny, finally blurted out, "Why do they get to leave? You're making me stay. Why aren't they suspects?"

Detective Breaux narrowed his eyes. "They aren't suspects because Carter is a sheriff and is aiding me in this investigation."

Kurt's eyes widened and he glanced at Carter. "You're a sheriff?"

"Yes," Carter replied.

Kurt glanced at Alaina, then back at Carter, and Alaina knew he wanted to ask what she'd done to rank a sheriff as an escort. But for once, he was wisely holding his tongue.

She studied Kurt for a moment—his stiff posture, the slight flush at the base of his neck, the way his fingers pulled at the bottom of his suit jacket. Maybe she was wrong. Maybe Kurt wasn't being wise at all.

Maybe he was scared.

ALAINA WAS SILENT as they crossed the parking lot to Carter's truck, and he wondered what was going through her mind. If it was anything like his own, so much was whirling through there that she couldn't gain focus on any one thing. Given Alaina's friendship with Emily and her own personal risk, she should be on the verge of cracking, but that was the last thing he needed. What he needed was for her to stay strong and alert.

They hopped in the truck and he started the engine and turned on the air-conditioning. "Are you all right?" he asked her.

She didn't respond immediately and he could see it took a second for her to process his question. Wherever she was in her head, it was miles away from here.

"No," she finally said. "I don't think I'm all right at all. What is going on, Carter? None of this makes sense."

She threw up her hands in frustration. "Every hour that passes, we add another layer to the puzzle, but all of them are foggy and none of them fit together. I'm beginning to think they're not related at all—that we have several different things happening and we're trying to force them to fit because then one answer would fix it all. Maybe it's just not that simple."

"Maybe it's not, but our process would be the same whether everything is related or not."

"I guess," she said, sounding totally defeated.

Carter struggled to find something to say to make things better, but for the first time in his life, he was at a complete loss. He didn't have the words to comfort her and he cared too much to walk away.

"Would you like to go by your place while we're in Baton Rouge?" he asked. "I noticed you didn't bring a lot of stuff with you. Maybe you want to pick up a few things?"

She perked up a little. "It would be nice to have more work clothes and some books. I always bought them thinking I'd get around to reading but never had the time."

"Well, you do now. Point me in the right direction and we'll make a stop before heading back to Calais."

She gave him a small smile. "Thanks. I know you're trying to make me feel better. It's working. Maybe that will make *you* feel better."

He smiled. "Maybe."

She directed him downtown to a high-rise condominium complex. Carter studied the complex as she entered her security code and they walked through the foyer to the elevators. The construction was fairly new and high-end. Marble floors, antique tables with crystal displayed and a giant painting hung in the entry.

It didn't surprise him. Alaina was an up-and-coming attorney with the best firm in the city. Her home would reflect her status and, likely, a nice salary. For some reason, this bothered him.

Maybe it was because her home was one more indicator that Alaina LeBeau was not a good fit for him or his life.

He'd be the first to admit that he grew bored sometimes with the slower pace of Calais, but he loved the town and had no desire to return to the city. The politics, lack of personnel and lack of funding were constant struggles for any large police department, and those things had grown to frustrate him so much that he could no longer effectively do his job.

He needed to be where he felt he could make a difference. In Calais, he spent more time chasing poachers and drunks than murderers, but that was okay, and it served the citizens of the town he'd sworn to protect. In Calais, everything he did mattered. In New Orleans, it seemed nothing he did mattered.

They exited the elevator on the tenth floor and walked down a wide hallway all the way to the end, where Alaina unlocked the door of a corner unit. But as soon as she pushed the door open, Carter knew things were very wrong.

A small cry escaped her before she stumbled back into him. Over her shoulder he could clearly see what caused her reaction. He put his hands on her shoulders and eased by her and into the condo.

Pictures had been torn off the walls. Her furniture slashed, the contents spilling out onto the floor. From his vantage point, he could see into the kitchen and the story was the same—the drawers had been pulled from their slots, every cabinet open and the contents of both strewn across the floor.

Alaina stepped next to him and stared at the damage. Her face was pale and she brought one shaky hand up to her mouth. She shuffled one foot forward and it connected with a broken lamp. She reached over, but before she could lift the lamp, he stopped her.

"Don't touch anything. He probably didn't leave prints, but the forensics team needs to try anyway."

She straightened back up. "One more useless puzzle piece."

She backed away and walked out of the condo. He stared after her, unable to think of a single word of comfort. He was simply all out.

AFTER SPENDING an exhausting two hours with the police and building security, then another trying to put her condo back to any semblance of normal, Alaina was more than ready to return to Calais. Wire on stairs and creepy specters were starting to seem tame in comparison to the things happening in Baton Rouge.

The forensics team had lifted prints, but Alaina would bet anything that when the results were in, the prints would belong only to her and those invited into her home. Despite an extensive review of all the contents, she'd been unable to find a single item missing even though jewelry of reasonable value was in clear boxes in the top drawer of her dresser. Nor had any of the electronics been touched.

It seemed as if whoever had broken in only wanted to create a mess, perhaps hoping to make her stressed or anxious—no one was sure. Unlike the vandalism on Everett's car, the perpetrator left no note behind this time, so they were left to only speculation. The day had exhausted Alaina to the point that even conjecture was beyond her maxed-out mind.

They'd just climbed into Carter's truck when his cell phone rang. He answered the call, then frowned. Alaina felt her heart drop, unsure she could take more bad news.

"We'll be there in five minutes," he said and hung up the phone.

"Emily?" All she could manage was the name, but she knew Carter would understand the question.

"No. They've found Steven Adams. He's at the police station right now for questioning. Detective Breaux wants us to listen in on the interrogation—see if anything sticks out to you."

Alaina let out a breath of relief that nothing more had transpired with Emily. "Do you think he could be behind it all?"

Carter frowned. "I wish I could say yes, but apparently, his alibi is tight for the time Emily was attacked this morning."

"Alibis can be paid for."

"He was in the drunk tank on the north side of the city until this afternoon."

"Damn."

"Yeah, that's what I was thinking but not as polite."

"Another dead end. If he was in the drunk tank last night, he couldn't have been breaking windows at the big mansion of horror in Calais either."

"No." Carter turned onto the boulevard and glanced over at her, frowning. "How well do you know Kurt McGraw? I know you worked with him, but what do you know about him other than his job?"

She shrugged. "He's the spoiled, only child hailing from a family of Ivy League–educated career politicians, most of whom are raging drunks and unapologetic cheaters. The firm spends a lot of gratis time making deals to get them off drunk driving convictions or to cheaply rid them of wives they wish to trade in on a newer model."

"They sound like lovely people. Is Kurt carrying on the drunken political tradition?"

"I'm pretty sure he's got the drunken part down—he seems to be mentally stuck in frat boy mode even though college was years ago. He's made no noise about politics as of yet, but I'm sure his family will push for it as soon as one of them wants to retire."

"You said he got the promotion you should have—what was that about?"

She gave him a quick rundown of the situation.

"So Kurt's family connections and the Warren case were used to pass you over?"

"That pretty much sums it up."

"I'm sorry about that."

"Thanks, but I think it might have been the best thing for me."

"Really? Why?"

"If I'm being honest with myself, I haven't been satisfied with my work for a long time, but if I'd gotten the partnership, I would never have left. This way, I can take some time and figure out what I really want to do."

"And then the inheritance dropped in your lap."

She nodded. "It seemed like a good opportunity to close myself away from the rush of the city, relax until I grew bored and do a lot of quiet contemplation on my future."

"Ha. How's that working out for you?"

"Yeah, well…I guess if I think about it all, it's still the best thing. Look how easily someone got to Emily and broke into my condo. In Baton Rouge, I'd have been an easy target. At least Calais throws some curveballs."

She looked over at him and smiled. "And in Calais, I have you instead of an overworked, spread-too-thin department."

He frowned. "I talked to the forensics team when you were going over the contents of your bedroom. They were going to do a more thorough check, but there doesn't appear to be any signs of a break-in."

She sucked in a breath. "How is that possible? They don't think I trashed my own home, do they? Besides, there are security pads everywhere. How could someone even get in the building and up to my floor without knowing the codes?"

"They don't think you did it yourself. But either someone is very good at picking locks and hacking security systems or they had a key and the codes. Does anyone have a key except you?"

"The building manager and maintenance, but other than that, no. All of my extended family is in other states and I'm not close enough to anyone in Baton Rouge to give them a key to my place."

"Did you ever leave your keys lying around at work?"

"I'm sure I did, but I don't see…" A thought flashed through her mind and she lost concentration.

"Something just occurred to you," Carter said.

"Kurt has a friend who lives in my building. I've seen him entering the elevators before. We're supposed to go down and let in our guests, but he was alone."

"His friend probably gave him the code so that he didn't have to go down to meet him."

"Probably. But it doesn't make sense. Why would Kurt be upset over the Warren case? That case guaranteed him the partnership."

"I don't know, but what I do know is that he had access to your building and likely your keys, he could have overheard Emily's call to you from the law office, and he was in Emily's hospital room when she coded. If he's not involved, he has the worst luck and timing of any individual in the world."

She clenched the door handle until her pulse pounded in her fingertips. Could her lazy and ineffective former coworker really be behind all this terror? "Why didn't the police tell me about their suspicions back at the condo?"

"They want to remove the lock from the door and do a more extensive search before making that final assessment. A fact like that can change the entire focus of an investigation and given all the seemingly connected issues and the fact that the perp is clearly willing to do physical harm, the police are going to make darn sure this investigation is clean and one hundred percent accurate."

Slowly, she let out the breath and released her grip on the door handle. "You're right. It's my job to know you're right. Why can't I focus?"

"Because your job has never been personal."

She looked over at him. "How did you get so smart?"

"My mom would tell you it's because of her."

She smiled. "Having met your mom, I think I'll agree."

He reached over and squeezed her hand. "We're going to figure this out. I'm not going to rest until I do."

A feeling of warmth ran through her and for the first time all day, she felt like things would ultimately be all right. What was it about Carter that made her feel as if he had the answers? As if his presence was all that was required to right her world? She'd never had such a strong connection with another person.

Except her mother.

CARTER LOOKED THROUGH the one-way glass into the interrogation room at Steven Adams. He was clearly hungover and more than a little angry at being dragged from one police department to another when he'd been expecting to walk free this afternoon. The only place he'd admitted to being in the past twenty-four hours was jail. The police already had proof of the bar where he'd gotten drunk, but his lips were sealed, even about that.

"He's not going to tell us anything," Carter said. "Either he's responsible for part of the stuff that's happened or he's responsible for none of it but is happy it's occurring. Either way, he's not going to assist in an investigation."

Alaina sighed. "Especially given who's being targeted."

"Exactly."

"There's nothing we can contribute here. I think we should head back to Calais and assess the situation at the house. We have to make it possible for you to stay there safely, and I want to alert everyone in town to be on the lookout for anything out of sorts. Calais residents don't take kindly to someone threatening one of their own."

"I'm a stranger."

"Maybe that's true now, but your mother wasn't, and a lot of people remember her fondly. Besides, no man worth his salt likes to see a woman harassed, regardless of his feelings toward her."

"The Southern-gentleman thing?"

"I'd like to believe just a gentleman thing. Let's get out of here," he said.

As they exited the viewing room, Detective Breaux came down the hall toward them. "We found a can of spray paint that matches that used on Winstrom's car in Adams's garage. The can was still in a bag from Carl's Hardware along with the receipt for two cans charged to Adams's credit card. No sign of the missing can anywhere in the garage or house."

"What about his wife?"

"She's thrilled we found him alive and swears she knows nothing about the paint. Her fingerprints aren't on them, the bag or the receipt, so it's possible she's telling the truth."

"So what's your take on it?" Carter asked.

Detective Breaux shrugged. "Gut instinct? I think

Adams went on a bender and spray-painted Winstrom's car, but I won't make a guess on any of the other things, except the attack on Ms. Jensen this morning. There's no way that could have been him."

"What about Larry Colbert? Anyone get a line on him yet?"

"No, but I think his wife is hiding something. When we questioned her before, it was only about the vandalism to Winstrom's car. Now that the investigation has escalated to attempted murder, maybe she'll be compelled to talk."

"True," Carter agreed, "especially if what she's hiding gives him an alibi."

"That's what I'm thinking," Detective Breaux said.

"Well, if you don't need anything else from us, we're going to head back to Calais and work on securing Alaina's house. Let me know when you come up with something."

Detective Breaux nodded. "And if you think of anything or you have any more issues in Calais, let me know."

"Will do," Carter said and they exited the police station.

"Did you tell Detective Breaux about Kurt having access to my building?" Alaina asked as they pulled out of the parking lot.

"Yeah. He's going to be looking at Kurt very closely, but given his political connections, also very carefully."

Alaina sighed. "Money and power complicate everything."

"Depends on which side of the coin you're on. For Kurt, it makes things easier."

"Very true." She looked out the windshield, her brow scrunched in concentration, then frowned. "Opportunity is there, but what I don't have a line on at all is motive. If we assume the same person who hurt Emily is the one harassing me, I can't think of any reason that Kurt would have for doing so. He got the partnership. I resigned from the firm. Why bother with me when I'm no longer a factor?"

"I don't know." Carter's jaw flexed involuntarily. Those were the hardest three words he'd ever spoken. Never in his life had he wanted something as badly as he wanted to fix this situation for Alaina. And instead, he was experiencing another first—not being able to think of a single thing to make it better. So far, all of his attempts had been futile or produced more questions.

Maybe you're too close.

The thought ripped through his mind and he clenched the steering wheel, not wanting to think about all the implications that came along with admitting that statement was true. The irony of the situation hit him full force. When William had asked him to check up on Alaina as a favor, he'd been peeved at the inconvenience, certain he'd butt heads with the city lawyer. Instead, the opposite had happened and he found himself in the impossible position of caring about someone who was destined to leave in a matter of weeks. The first day he'd driven to the house to meet Alaina, he'd been mentally tallying the days until she left.

Now, he wished that tally was bigger.

CARTER THREW his cell phone onto the kitchen countertop and turned to stare out the window into the swamp. Alaina could see his jaw flex, even from her vantage point on the other side of the counter. The call had been from Detective Breaux, but from Carter's reaction, it wasn't good news. What if something else had happened to Emily?

"What's wrong?" she asked, her voice cracking.

He turned back around to face her and immediately

looked contrite. "I'm sorry. I didn't mean to worry you. Emily is still in a coma, but her vitals are steady and there's a guard in front of her room and another sitting with the nurse at the station tonight. No one is allowed by except the on-duty doctor, and only the nurse can approve him."

She blew out a breath of relief. "I'm glad they stepped up security."

"Me, too."

"So what *is* wrong?"

He threw his hands in the air. "Nothing's *wrong,* really. It's the lack of forward movement that's frustrating me."

"I guess Detective Breaux didn't make any headway with Kurt?"

"Ha. He lawyered up and refused to talk. Then the mayor called the police captain and interrupted dinner with his family to explain to the captain just how unhappy he was that such a fine young man was being railroaded so that the police could look like they were doing their job."

"Figures. I expected as much."

"Yeah, well, unless you get video of Kurt McGraw committing a crime, you're not likely to get anywhere."

She sighed. "Probably not. No progress with Colbert's wife either?"

"She completely clammed up. Told him to arrest her or get off her porch, then went on to say that if he arrested her, she still wasn't speaking except to her attorney."

"Do you think Colbert's behind it all? Maybe he and Adams were in it together."

"Anything's possible. Her refusal to tell where her husband is certainly doesn't make him look all that innocent. But then, she's not likely to care what he's suspected of when she blames the firm for her daughter's death."

"And so I'm in the same position now that I have been

since the beginning." Alaina said what she knew he was thinking but didn't want to voice. The reality was, as long as the attacker was roaming free, she was at risk. The Baton Rouge police didn't have the manpower to send armed guards to Calais, and given the situation with her condo, she wasn't safe there either.

Carter blew out a breath. "I know I said we'd stay at my place tonight, but I was thinking… No, never mind."

"You want to set a trap for him."

His eyes widened.

She gave him a small smile. "I *did* work with cops, remember?"

"It was a moment of weakness and a really bad thought. Forget it."

"I don't think so." A million different scenarios ran through her mind, and she categorized and filed them all just like she used to when she was working a case.

"We both know this won't stop until he gets what he wants or he gets caught," she continued. "Even if he guessed where I was hiding, he's not going to risk coming after me at your place. It's too small and I don't think he's desperate…yet. But if we made it look like I was here alone, then he might take a shot at me here. With both of us ready for him, we have a chance to end this now. Tonight."

Carter shook his head. "You're not a cop. I can't ask you to do that."

"Who's asking?"

"Even if you're volunteering, it's my responsibility to tell you no. I'm supposed to protect you, not elicit your help doing my job."

"Fine, but I have no intention of leaving here tonight. So unless you plan on arresting me or leaving me here alone, I don't see that you have much choice."

"It's too dangerous," he said, but Alaina could tell his argument was waning.

"So what's less dangerous—waiting for Detective Breaux to catch Colbert? And so what if he does? He has no proof to tie him to any of this and neither do we. He'd walk and you know it. And if it's not him, then we're really at a disadvantage because everyone's concentrating on finding the wrong person."

She threw her hands in the air. "For all we know, it could be your disgruntled cook harassing me here and something completely different going on in Baton Rouge. The only way to know for sure who's after me is to catch him in the act. Do you want to do that now or wait until I leave Calais and then run the risk of my having to deal with the same thing somewhere else?"

He stiffened and Alaina could tell she'd struck a big nerve. Good. That was exactly what she'd intended. She didn't like the situation any more than he did and she was aware of the danger, but she also knew she had more of an advantage here with Carter's help than she did anywhere else. Looking over your shoulder every minute of every day was no way to live. This was supposed to be the start of a new life and as things currently stood, someone was preventing that from happening.

One way or another, it was going to stop.

Finally, he sighed. "I know you're right, but I hate it. You will never know how badly I hate it."

She walked over to him and placed her hand on his arm. "I know you hate it, but I trust you. I can't be assured of that with anyone else going forward. And in some screwed-up way, it feels to me like it has to happen here. Like I have to tie up all loose strings to the past before I can move forward."

He looked at her and she could see in his expression

that he got it, even though he didn't like it. He leaned over and kissed her gently on the lips.

"I won't let anything happen to you," he promised before wrapping his arms around her and drawing her close to his chest.

"I know you won't," she said, but at that moment, her real fear was not from the unknown assailant—it was from her feelings for Carter.

Chapter Seventeen

They waited until dark. It would be easier for Carter to slip back into the house unnoticed in the inky black of night. A storm was brewing overhead, but it was supposed to hold off until after midnight. With any luck, this would all be over by then.

Alaina stood at the front door with Carter as he prepared to leave, trying to hold back the anxiety that was creeping in. Setting a trap had sounded like a great idea in the bright light of day, but now that it was in motion, a million worries she hadn't thought of before tumbled through her mind.

"Get up to the bedroom as soon as you lock this door," Carter said, his voice low. "Keep your pistol in your hand, ready to fire. Amos is waiting for me at the café. I'll exchange trucks with him and he'll spend the evening having pot roast at my mom's. No one should be able to make out who's driving in the dark. I'll make my way back through the swamp from his cabin and scale the balcony to the bedroom. The rope is hidden in the vines and can't be seen without digging for it. You stay put, and unless it's me, be ready to shoot."

Alaina nodded. They'd gone over the plan a million times—every detail of every movement. She knew it was solid and she trusted Carter to protect her.

"It shouldn't take more than thirty minutes for me to get back," Carter whispered.

"I know," she said, but those thirty minutes were the part that bothered Alaina the most. One thousand eight hundred excruciatingly long seconds alone in the house, locked up in the bedroom, fingers wrapped around her nine millimeter.

He studied her for a moment, then leaned over and dropped his lips to hers. The brush of his skin on hers set her body on fire and reenergized her in a way mere words could never have done. When this was over—really over—she had a lot of thinking to do about Carter Trahan.

He broke off the kiss and opened the front door, then with one final long look at her, he disappeared into the building storm.

Alaina grabbed her pistol from the entry table and hurried upstairs. She did a quick check under the bed and in the closet, then locked the bedroom door behind her and turned off the overhead light before slipping into the corner behind the school desks.

The light from the kerosene lamp on the dresser cast a dim glow over the room, reaching almost to the corners. She could easily make out the bed pillows, lined under the covers to look like someone sleeping. When Carter returned, she'd unlock the bedroom door and pretend to go to the bathroom. If they were right, the assailant would choose that moment to try and lure her downstairs or sneak into her room.

Either way, Carter would be ready. If the assailant entered the room, he'd take him down. If the assailant attempted to draw her downstairs, Carter would use the servant's stairwell to slip down into the kitchen and try to ferret him out in the darkness. Alaina was to remain secure in the bathroom until Carter came to get her. It wasn't the best plan and certainly not the safest, but it was what they had to work with.

They'd carefully checked every square inch of the servants' stairs and the doors. Squeaky hinges had been oiled and loose stairs had been secured, allowing for silent passage. They'd released the bathroom window from the many layers of paint that had sealed it shut, and stored a climbing rope in the linen closet. If things went bad, she would scramble out of the window and drive to Calais for help.

In the meantime, she was going to pray that things didn't go bad.

She glanced down at her watch and struggled for patience. Only three minutes had passed since Carter left. She had at least another long, agonizing twenty-seven minutes to go before he'd make his way up the balcony and she'd let him in through the patio doors. Thousands of opportunities for something to go horribly wrong and even more opportunity for her to imagine things going horribly wrong.

For the first time in her life, the reality of what it truly meant to be a law enforcement officer struck her. She'd always respected the work cops did, even though they'd butted heads at times, and she'd never thought it was easy. But she'd also never imagined it being this hard. Surely, they all had their nerves cauterized during training. Or perhaps beta-blockers were issued right along with pistols and handcuffs.

Her left foot began to tingle and she shifted her weight to her right side. It would be much easier if she sat, but sitting was hardly optimal if the need to flee came about. A dull ache, courtesy of an old track-and-field injury, started up in her right foot but she promptly ignored it. Heat and ice could come later, when she was certain she could sit still and be safe.

As the minutes ticked away, the events of the past year played through her mind. So much had changed—some for the better and some not so much. A year ago, if anyone had told her she'd be in a spooky mansion, hiding in a bedroom and trying to catch a criminal, she would have had them committed. A year ago, if anyone had told her that her heart and body would be longing for a hunky small-town sheriff, she would have said they were crazy. A year ago, her life was so much simpler.

And so empty.

She stiffened at that thought. Had she really been so focused on her career that she'd never stopped to ask herself if she even wanted it? Had she used it to shield herself from forming the close personal relationships that were far more important than a job?

She blew out a breath. Her two weeks in Calais were supposed to have been a time of reflection and decision making, but she hadn't seen these huge revelations coming.

Or Carter Trahan.

Suddenly, a dull thud sounded somewhere in the house and she froze. One glance at her watch told her it was too soon for Carter to be back. Besides, Carter would enter the house from the bedroom balcony. The noise she'd heard had definitely come from inside. With her. Where she was all alone.

Stay calm. Remember the plan.

Yeah, right. The plan included Carter being here.

She gripped her pistol with both hands and aimed it over the desks and at the door, her hands shaking even when propped on the desk seat. If anyone came through that door, she would empty her magazine into them. Given that they'd have to pick the lock or break down the door to get through it, no one could fault her for the shooting. It would definitely be a case of self-defense.

She took a deep breath and slowly blew it out, mentally running through the case law for self-defense shootings. Silently reciting the cases and rulings calmed her, and the shaking in her hands decreased. She took another breath and continued her mental recital.

The creak of a floorboard in the hallway right outside her room echoed through the still night air like a scream. She flung her hand over her mouth, stifling a cry. Seconds later, the door handle jiggled and she put her hand back on the pistol, her finger positioned on the trigger.

Squeeze, don't pull.

She'd done it a million times at the gun range, shooting paper targets with deadly accuracy. Now it was time to put all that training to use. All she had to do was imagine that paper target and fire. She could do this.

Then the jiggling stopped and she heard the hinges of a door squeak. He must have entered one of the other rooms off the hallway, but why? She and Carter had checked every square inch of this room. No servants' passage existed. The only way in and out was the main bedroom door and the patio.

A second later, she had her answer.

The roar of a gunshot seemed to shake the wall beside her. She screamed as splinters of wood pricked her neck and bare arms as the round broke through the paneling. Instinctively, she flung herself flat on the floor as another round pierced through the wall right where she'd been squatting.

She was a sitting duck. He could stand there firing as long as he had ammunition. Firing back would do her no good. Her nine millimeter wouldn't pierce two walls of paneling. Her only chance was to run for it.

Digging the toes of her tennis shoes into the wood floor, she pushed with her legs and pulled with her one free hand to drag herself over to the patio doors. Her heart thumped so strongly that it was like a hammer beating against the hardwood. A single bead of sweat ran down her forehead and directly into her eye, blurring her vision, and she clenched her pistol so tightly that her fingers began to ache.

Another shot rang out and hit the kerosene lamp on the dresser—shattering it and pitching her into complete darkness.

She took a breath and continued to push on. It couldn't be much farther now. And just when her calves started to cramp, her hand hit the bottom frame of the French doors. She slid her hand up the door, trying to keep her head low while fumbling for the lock. After what felt like an eternity, her fingers circled around the dead bolt and she turned it.

Two more shots fired and some of the glass panes on the doors shattered. Involuntarily, her hand jerked back and she had to force herself to reach up again for the doorknob. She closed her hand around it and pulled the door open wide enough to drag herself over the threshold. The broken glass dug into her palms and pierced through her T-shirt, cutting the sensitive skin on her chest and stomach.

She bit back a cry, trying not to give away her position in the room, and continued across the glass-littered threshold until she reached the balcony. Now came the really hard part. The rails of the balcony were too close together for her to fit through. She had to stand to get over the railing, and standing put her at huge risk for a lucky shot landing its mark.

Carter had left the rope tied to the post in the middle. All she had to do was jump up, grab that rope and scale down the plaster column to the patio below. Then she'd run like she'd never run before. Reaching behind her back, she stuck her pistol in her waistband holster. She'd need both hands for the rope.

She took a deep breath. *On three. One. Two. Three!*

She bolted up and reached for the rope. Panic washed over her when she couldn't find it in the thick vines circling the column. Another shot sounded and she felt it whizz by, inches from her head. She tore the vines from the column, digging for the rope in the pitch-dark night, holding in a cry of relief when her fingers finally wrapped around the coarse line.

Her relief disappeared as the door to the bedroom burst open and the light from a flashlight struck her directly in the face, blinding her. She ducked as another shot rang over her head. The blood rushed out of her head as she accepted the fact that this was how it would all end. She was out of options.

She cringed, waiting for the killing shot to hit her immobile body, but instead, a strangled cry came from inside the room. She saw the flashlight hit the floor and then looked up and saw what had caused the shooter to fumble.

The shimmering white figure of her mother hovered two feet above the bedroom floor, floating directly between her and the shooter.

She leaped up from the balcony and grabbed the railing, rolling her body over the top. A shot rang out and grazed the top of her arm before she let the railing go and dropped onto the patio below. Her left foot landed on a stone and twisted, wrenching her ankle, but she had no time to dwell on injuries. She ran into the swamp behind the patio as the shooter burst out onto the balcony behind her.

He fired off several shots, the bullets whizzing by her in the dense, black swamp. She pushed herself through the thick foliage as fast as it allowed, her thighs and calves burning from the strain. When she reached the path to Amos's cabin, she drew up short.

What the hell had just happened? By all rights, she should be dead on that balcony and would be if it hadn't been for her mother. Correction—her mother's ghost.

She shook her head, trying to clear the image of her mother, shimmering in light and hovering two feet above the floor, out of her mind. She'd deal with her thoughts on that later.

If there was a later.

Going to the caretaker's cabin was tempting, but it was no place to mount a defense. Surrounded by the snaking bayou, there was only one way out unless she wanted to dive into the alligator-infested water and swim for it.

She pulled her cell phone from her pocket and checked it, expecting nothing, given the dark storm clouds circling above. No signal. She put the phone away and pulled out her pistol. In the rustle of the brush in the stormy winds, she couldn't hear the sound of pursuit behind her, but that didn't mean he wasn't there somewhere, just waiting for a sound to indicate where she was hiding.

The moonlight peeked out from behind a cloud long enough for her to scan the path in both directions. The path was clear. She waited until the clouds rolled back over the moon, then hurried across the path into the foliage on the other side. Maybe the killer would stick to that side of the path, thinking she wouldn't cross it and go deeper into the swamp.

He was wrong.

CARTER PARKED HIS TRUCK behind a stretch of thick brush about a quarter mile from the house. He'd intended to park at the caretaker's cabin and make his way to the house by the path, but parking here saved him some of the drive and eliminated the possibility of being seen passing near the house. It would be a quick jog through the brush, skirting the road, and then a quick trip around the house to scale the balcony.

When he was halfway to the house, the first shot echoed in the distance.

He froze, certain he'd mistaken some other sound for a gunshot. But when the second shot fired—hollow and faint—he knew someone was firing a pistol inside the house. And for him to hear it this far out, it had to be high-caliber.

He leaped through the brush and onto the road in a dead run for the house, all plans of subversive maneuvers gone right out the window. As he ran, he said a silent prayer that Alaina had gotten out of the house or returned fire. It was possible he couldn't hear the nine millimeter at this distance.

And it's possible she had no chance to fire.

He forced the thought from his mind and pushed his legs harder to increase speed, not even hesitating when he ran through the gates and into the courtyard. He fumbled with the key to the front door and cursed before finally shoving the unlocked door open and peering inside.

The downstairs lights were still on, which surprised him, but made it easier to determine that he was alone—at least, it appeared that way. Before he could think of all the other possibilities, he dashed across the entry and up the stairs, clenching his pistol in his right hand. When he hit the landing, he saw the bullet holes through the bedroom door and his heart fell.

He raced into the bedroom without a thought of his own safety and slid to a stop in the empty room. The evidence of the struggle was everywhere—splintered wood, broken glass, the patio door that stood open. He ran to the patio and looked over, but there was no sign of her on the patio below. Clenching the rail, he peered into the pitch-black swamp, wondering which direction she'd taken and how far she'd already run.

Wondering if the killer had caught her.

He clenched the railing at the thought and felt something moist on his palm. He lifted it into the light and saw blood smeared on it. His heart fell once again. Had a bullet pierced her flawless skin or was it the killer's blood?

Using the blood-smeared hand, he vaulted over the balcony, still clutching his pistol in his other hand. As soon as his feet hit the stone patio, he collapsed and rolled, letting the tumbling motion absorb all the energy of the drop. Thorns from the overgrown rose bushes pressed into his skin, but he barely noticed as he bounced to his feet, pausing only long enough to pull a penlight from his pocket.

It took only seconds to identify the broken branches and compacted brush and he set off after Alaina, hoping he found her before the killer did.

ALAINA PUSHED THROUGH the thick swamp, pausing only long enough to make sure she hadn't strayed too far from the path. Her sense of direction was better than most and she was managing to progress back toward the house while maintaining a distance of twenty or so feet from the path. Unless he was a skilled tracker, the killer wouldn't notice where she'd entered the swamp on the other side of the path. She figured he would assume she ran down the path toward the house and would pursue her that way.

She was tempted to set off down that path at a dead run. Even though she hadn't been competitively on a track in ages, she knew she could outrun the vast majority of people she came in contact with. But even at her best, she couldn't outrun ammunition. She had to be smart and agile—her life depended on it.

So she pushed farther through the swamp, every second seeming like an hour. The night air had stilled—the calm before the storm—causing the humidity to soar. Sweat formed on her forehead and stung the cuts on her hand when she wiped it away. It couldn't be much farther, she kept telling herself. Her pace away from the house was much faster, but she'd been trekking back toward the house far longer than she'd run away.

Finally, a flicker of light pierced through the thick foliage. She inched closer to the path and light from the front entry creeping across the circular drive. Silently, she cursed at her car, parked directly in the brightest path of light. When she and Carter had made their plans that evening, it had seemed like a good idea to park her car right next to the house, where she'd left it every night before. Unfortunately, it was in the one spot that risked the most exposure.

Not only was the entire area surrounding the car illuminated by the entry light, but it was also impossible to reach it without crossing the circular drive, leaving her an easy target for even the worst of marksmen.

She scanned the drive, looking for any sign of movement, any shadow that didn't fit the angle of the house or bushes, but it appeared clear. The silence was almost deafening, as if the swamp was holding its breath right along with her. She felt her jeans pocket for the electronic key to her SUV. The technology allowed her to enter and start her vehicle without removing the key from her pocket, so no time was lost fumbling for keys, but still she hesitated.

The quiet unnerved her.

If the wind blew through the brush and the insects picked up their tune again, she would feel better, but right now, it was like a giant spotlight was on her—like everything was waiting and watching her next move. She mentally marked the distance between her hiding spot and the SUV. It was only twenty yards, but it had to be the longest twenty yards she'd ever seen.

Still, the killer hadn't passed her on the path, which she hoped meant he was still behind her somewhere, looking for her in the swamp. The longer she waited to make her move, the more opportunity he had to catch up with her. She clenched her gun and sprang out of the bushes, then sprinted for her car. With each stride, her hopes increased until finally, she slid to a stop next to the driver's door.

Before she could grab the handle, a gunshot boomed in the still night air, and the driver's side window exploded. She grabbed the door handle.

"I wouldn't do that if I were you," a voice she recognized sounded behind her.

A wave of dizziness washed over her as she slowly turned around to find Everett Winstrom III standing ten feet away, his forty-five leveled at her.

"You?" she gasped. "But I don't understand…"

He stared at her, his disgust clear. "You couldn't leave it alone, could you? I thought if you were passed over for the partnership, you'd resign and it would all be over with. I thought the past could be left in the past where it belongs, and I could move forward with my own political aspirations. But you had to keep digging. Your meddling will get Emily killed. You shouldn't have involved her."

"I didn't! I don't know what's going on. I swear!"

"That may be the case, but you know enough to keep digging. I know you, Alaina. You won't let it go. The only way I'm safe is if you're dead. And poor Emily…what a shame. The girl had promise."

"You're mad."

He laughed and her skin prickled.

"Oh, I'm completely sane," he said. "I know exactly what I want and you're not going to get in the way."

She stared at him, the man she'd worked with every week for the past seven years. How had she missed his instability? How had she failed to notice ambition so big that it was eating away at his sanity?

"At least tell me what all this is about," she said. "I deserve to know why you're going to kill me."

"No, I don't think so. I think you deserve to die just the way you are now, especially given all the trouble you've caused."

This was it. She was going to die before her life had even begun. All those years focused on a career that didn't matter instead of forming relationships that did. Now that she was on the verge of what could be the most important relationship she'd ever had, she was going to die.

He pointed the gun directly at her head and smiled as his finger whitened on the trigger.

When the shot came, her knees collapsed and she slumped against her SUV, her eyes clenched shut. It took her a second to realize she hadn't been hit. She opened her eyes just in time to see Carter race across the driveway toward her. He paused long enough to pick up Everett's gun, then rushed over and dropped down beside her.

"Are you all right? Were you hit?"

She threw herself into his arms and he placed Everett's gun on the ground and held her tightly. She felt the soft stroke of his free hand running across her hair and in the middle of her back, the hard metal from his gun pressed into her as he held her.

It suddenly struck her that this exact moment personified everything that was Carter Trahan—soft and caring but ruthless and hard when protecting those he cared about.

Right there, kneeling in the driveway—her hands and chest still stinging from glass cuts, her legs already cramping from her run, her body drenched in sweat and her mind only moments from believing she was going to die—it was the most perfect moment of her entire life.

CARTER CLUTCHED ALAINA, never wanting to let her go. He couldn't believe how close he'd come to losing her. If not for her intelligence—her bravery and ability to think cool under pressure—he had no doubt this all would have ended tragically.

She was unlike any woman he'd ever known. He kissed her ear and squeezed her tighter. All those years in New Orleans—with millions of beautiful women living in and passing through the city each year—and he'd had to return to his tiny hometown to find perfection.

"I thought I'd lost you," he whispered.

"I thought you had, too."

He pulled back a bit so that he could look down at her. "I wouldn't have been able to live with that. I don't know how or when it happened, but I don't want to be without you, Alaina."

Her eyes widened and filled with tears, and her bottom lip trembled. For a moment, he thought she was going to try to gently let him down—that she was going to tell him she cared but not as much as he did.

Then she leaned forward and pressed her lips to his. And he had his answer.

Chapter Eighteen

Alaina pulled packing tape over the last of the boxes in her Baton Rouge condo just as Carter opened the door and walked in. It had been a little over a week since her flight from Everett. She'd finished her two weeks in the old house without incident, not even a ghostly one.

That part made her a bit sad, but maybe her mother had appeared to help her and that was all she could manage from another plane of existence. The evil-looking specter that had appeared over her bed that first night had never returned, and as time passed, Alaina began to wonder if she'd imagined it.

"Is that the last of it?" Carter asked as he pulled a dolly in behind him.

"Last one," she said and smiled.

A month ago, if anyone had told her that she'd be selling off half of her belongings and packing the rest in boxes to move to a town so small it didn't even show on maps, she would have laughed. But now, she couldn't imagine any other life.

Of course, a life with Carter Trahan was hardly a consolation prize.

And she had plenty of time to decide what she wanted to do career-wise. For the time being, she was going to help William at his practice on an as-needed basis and continue her work with a couple of corporate clients in New Orleans who still wanted her to represent them in business matters, even though she'd left the firm.

Carter grabbed her around the waist with one arm and twirled her around as she laughed. Then he set her down and kissed her long and deep—reminding her of what she had in store that night and every other after it.

As he broke off the kiss and released her, he said, "Detective Breaux called while I was loading the boxes."

"Did they find anything?"

The Baton Rouge police had been trying to piece together the reason for Everett's attack on her and Emily. The intern had finally awakened and doctors expected her to make a full recovery. What no one expected was for her to be as shocked as Alaina to find out that Everett was behind the attack.

Emily overheard Everett and another partner arguing the day before she'd called Alaina. The partner was expressing his displeasure at Alaina being passed over for the partnership in favor of Kurt. Everett had cited her mistakes on the Warren case as his reason and said he was only protecting the firm. Emily had pulled the case file to read so that she could understand what construed a mistake when you'd won your case. She'd called Alaina to tell her about the argument and ask her why Everett felt she'd made a mistake.

That innocent phone call and copying the case file had unwittingly been her undoing.

So the Baton Rouge police, upon direction from Emily and Alaina, began a forensic search of all the law firm's records, trying to determine if someone had been deleting or altering them. The police had already been at it for a week.

Kurt had already confessed to giving Everett the passcode to Alaina's building, but he'd thought the senior partner only wanted to try and talk her out of leaving. Because Alaina always left her house key in her unlocked desk drawer, Everett could easily have swiped it at any time and made a copy for use in case he ever suspected she was on to him.

The only thing they hadn't figured out was how Everett got into the house in Calais, but Carter was determined not to rest until he had an answer.

"Oh, they found something all right," Carter said. "They found the answer to everything."

Alaina sucked in a breath. "Really? What is it? What did Everett think we knew?"

A flash of anger passed over Carter's face. "It was a piece of deleted video from when Warren Sr. and his son were in your conference room. The son admitted to molesting the girl and his father told him exactly what to say in the interview with you."

Her hand flew up to her mouth. "No! How could he? How could Everett delete that knowing he was risking putting a child predator back on the street?"

"He didn't care a whit about children. He was using the information to blackmail Warren Sr. into supporting an upcoming run for state senate. He had nothing to lose and everything to gain, especially because you were positioned nicely as the lead attorney to take the fall if something went south. Or I should say *when* something went south. He had to know that the kid would reoffend. They always do."

She slumped down into one of her dining room chairs. "That other girl didn't have to die."

"No, she didn't." He placed one hand on her shoulder. "But that is not on you."

"Tell that to the families."

"Detective Breaux already has. They are angry and sad, but they understand that you and Emily were Everett's victims, as well."

"What about Colbert? Did his wife ever give up his location?"

"Yeah. He had a nervous breakdown and was checked into a substance abuse facility. She knew the attacker couldn't have been him and wasn't about to tell the very people she held responsible for his condition."

Alaina sighed. "I don't blame her. The entire thing is so ugly."

"Yes, but it's in the past." He reached down and pulled her up into his arms. "*You* are very beautiful and I can't wait to have you making my life gorgeous every day."

She smiled. "Every day? I don't get a day off?"

"No. Sorry."

He lowered his lips to hers.

I'm not, she thought before losing herself in his arms.

* * * * *

Jana DeLeon's spine-tingling new miniseries,
MYSTERE PARISH: FAMILY INHERITANCE,
is just getting started.
Don't miss Danae LeBeau's story,
THE BETRAYED, available next month
wherever Harlequin Intrigue books are sold!

COMING NEXT MONTH from Harlequin® Intrigue®
AVAILABLE AUGUST 20, 2013

#1443 BRIDAL ARMOR
Colby Agency: The Specialists
Debra Webb
Thomas Casey's extreme black ops team is the best at recovering the worst situations. When thrust into the most dangerous situation of his career, can he recover his heart?

#1444 TASK FORCE BRIDE
The Precinct: Task Force
Julie Miller
A tough K-9 cop masquerades as the fiancé of a shy bridal-shop owner in order to protect her from the terrifying criminal who's hot on her trail.

#1445 GLITTER AND GUNFIRE
Shadow Agents
Cynthia Eden
Cale Lane is used to life-or-death battles. But when the former army ranger's new mission is to simply watch over gorgeous socialite Cassidy Sherridan, he follows orders.

#1446 BODYGUARD UNDER FIRE
Covert Cowboys, Inc.
Elle James
Recruited to join an elite undercover group, former army Special Forces soldier Chuck Bolton returns to Texas. And his first assignment is to protect his former fiancé...and the child he's never met.

#1447 THE BETRAYED
Mystere Parish: Family Inheritance
Jana DeLeon
Danae LeBeau thought she'd find answers when she returned to her childhood home, but someone doesn't like the questions she's asking. And the guy next door will stop at nothing to find out why.

#1448 MOST ELIGIBLE SPY
HQ: Texas
Dana Marton
After being betrayed by her own brother, can Molly Rogers trust an unknown soldier to save her and her son from ruthless smugglers who are out for blood?

You can find more information on upcoming Harlequin® titles, free excerpts and more at www.Harlequin.com.

REQUEST YOUR FREE BOOKS!
2 FREE NOVELS PLUS 2 FREE GIFTS!

HARLEQUIN®

INTRIGUE®

BREATHTAKING ROMANTIC SUSPENSE

HI13R

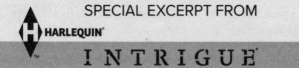
Read on for a sneak-peek of USA TODAY bestselling author Debra Webb's first installment of her brand-new COLBY AGENCY: THE SPECIALISTS series,

Bridal Armor

At the airport in Denver, Colby Agency spy Thomas Casey is intercepted by the only woman who ever made him think twice about his unflinching determination to remain unattached...

She flashed an overly bright smile and handed him a passport. "That's you, right?"

He opened it and, startled, gazed up at her. "Who are you?"

"You know me," she murmured, leaning closer. "Thomas."

His eyes went wide as he recognized her voice under the disguise.

"I need you." The words were out, full of more truth than she cared to admit regarding their past, present and, quite possibly, their immediate future.

He nodded once, all business, and fell in beside her as she headed toward an employee access. She refused to look back, though she could feel Grant closing in as the door locked behind them.

"This way."

"Tell me what's going on, Jo."

She ignored the ripple of awareness that followed his using her given name. It wasn't the reaction she'd expected. Thomas always treated everyone with efficient professionalism. Except for that one notable, extremely personal, incident years ago.

"I'll tell you everything just as soon as we're out of here." She checked her watch. They had less than five minutes before the cabbie she'd paid to wait left in search of another fare. "Keep up. We have to get out of the area before the roads are closed." She'd taken precautions, given herself options, but no one could prepare for a freak blizzard.

"Are you in trouble?"

"Yes." On one too many levels, she realized. But it was too late to back out now. If she didn't follow through, someone more objective would take over the investigation. Based on what she'd seen, she didn't think that was a good idea.

Moving forward, she hoped some deep-seated instinct would kick in, making him curious enough to cooperate with her.

"Jo, wait."

Would the day ever come when his voice didn't create that shiver of anticipation? "No time."

"I need an explanation."

"And I'll give you one when we're away from the airport."

Can Jo be trusted or is it a trap?
Then again, nothing is too dangerous for these agents...
except falling in love.

Don't miss

Bridal Armor

by Debra Webb

Book one in the

COLBY AGENCY: THE SPECIALISTS SERIES

Available August 20, edge-of-your-seat romance,
only from Harlequin® Intrigue®!